AXO LOTL

ROADKILL

A Novel

Helene Hegemann

Translated by Katy Derbyshire

corsair

Constable & Robinson Ltd
55–56 Russell Square
London WC1B 4HP
www.constablerobinson.com

First published in the UK by Corsair,
an imprint of Constable & Robinson Ltd, 2012

A copy of the British Library Cataloguing in
Publication data is available from the British Library

ISBN: 978-1-84901-054-2 (paperback)
ISBN: 978-184901-888-3 (ebook)

Printed and bound in the EU

1 3 5 7 9 10 8 6 4 2

MIX
Paper from
responsible sources
FSC® C018072
FSC
www.fsc.org

For Lilly Sternberg

'We love to entertain you'
(Pro7)

OK, so it's night, and once again that grapple with death, the snatches of fearful sleep, my bedroom shaking with daemonic orchestras and all the burglars' voices from the backyard continually screaming my name. Not the noise of city roads and not the moans of great ugly giants in agony, unbandaged. Only the dark's spinets, the howling in my head, the arrhythmic drumming – oh shit. In the old days it all got spewed up in finest adolescent style and now it's seriously intense literature.

I wake at 16:30, disorientated and wrapped in a duvet cover, primarily bored by myself. I cower. Laurel wreaths woven out of blood kind of flow out of my right ear. Something flashes before my eyes and I recognize it as high-society grotesquery: two cigarettes, two lines of Ritalin snorted through a till receipt instead of a banknote for reasons of hygiene, pulverized Parmesan and a nervous breakdown assuming worrying proportions, presumably the K-hole. For months now I've been having the wildest cancer diagnosis dreams – something deeper than nightmares, where I wake up screaming because there are so many thoughts that you can't distinguish your own from other people's. What with all my gastric excesses coupled with panic attacks, I feel like launching myself from my third-floor window. But instead I switch on trashy TV and watch a great nature documentary. It's like some amazing televisual event. All of a sudden there's this alert jackal, and then there's a counter-shot of a herd of meerkats, and then they get all ripped to shreds by the jackal in close-up and the viewer overflows with love and thinks: yup, those freaking meerkats really do look so incredibly dumb, they just, like, don't deserve anything better than getting eaten.

I can either wank off to high-quality hardcore porn or stare at my fingernails and then in the mirror. My dermal appendages have grown into intercrusted eczema and my eyelashes are breaking off.

At that moment, silence falls again.

A trace of social acceptability, no hardtechno track drilling through it any more, just a sobering early fucking summer wind. I didn't go to school. Five minutes before breaktime I was struggling out from beneath the covers in mortal fear, my heart racing and pain crashing against my skull with every step, even though at that point in time I ought to have been thinking:

All right, today I'll make contact with a tomato for a change. I have to remove it from the sandwich my re-sponsible parental unit has placed it in for my school lunch.

An hour after hometime I'm standing in front of the mirror, my legs spreadeagled, in the vacant flow of memories of last night's sweat-soaked gimpish grin and the power of those repetitive dance beats that take on a life of their own.

I want to build a children's home in Afghanistan and own loads of clothes. I don't just need food and a roof

2

over my head; I need three villas with titanium white fixtures and fittings, up to eleven prostitutes every day and a Soviet-style Chanel suit swathing me in plush golden twenties chic. Then there'd be no such words as *self-awareness* and *borderline* any more. And no one who pretends to know you better than you do yourself – all that would count then is money. Now we're getting there. I suddenly notice everyone gaping at me. I go out on the balcony with my fifth cigarette. I'll just drink and drink until the money's all GONE. Right now my existence consists entirely of dizzy spells and the fact that it's been half ripped to shreds by a hyper-real installation of Vaselined tits blurred by Rohypnol.

I say, 'As soon as we begin doing something for others, we release ourselves from the prison inside of us. Alice hates herself, but that's what's so awesome: I can see she's losing it and increasingly destroying herself. I'm so scared I can't think any more. I'll do anything to still have the privilege of knowing you. It's no big deal if you don't want to fuck me any more. You've disappeared out of my life now. It's not as if I can abuse myself here the whole time with self-reflection and self-torment; I don't know, there must be something else, like an irrational moment, one of those moments when you give me that fixed look with your colourless eyes. I can always see you're just working out how many people are standing between us right now. Do you remember? How we always had to work out how many metres apart we were? And how I told you at some point, when we were alone at last, what perfection that was for me? Those moments when we looked at the sea – they were so perfect that I didn't have to savour them. I can tell I'm going crazy. I can't distinguish any more between dreaming and what

3

you call reality. Because everything feels the same. The wind, your skin, everything three-dimensional.'

Under the shower, drops patter down in slow motion, aspiring to spherical form through the influence of surface tension.

Against the general assumption, a droplet of water is at no time drop-shaped, that two-dimensional shite: round at one end and pointed at the other. I tug a turquoise sheet out of the dirty washing to dry myself; it's spent the past two months in a large basket in the company of two puke-encrusted items of clothing. Is it a stranger's puke – someone who caught me by surprise in a highly frequented unisex toilet? Is it my puke? Does that bring me closer to myself in some way? It really looks like I'm starting to forget the most essential details.

I'm standing in the hallway, terminally depressed, on a carpet laid for some inexplicable reason in the dim and distant past, and it's kind of greyish green, it's dirty, it's covered with burn marks. Oh God, it's all so awful.

1. I've lost my patchworked personal history which is marked out by anal sex, tears and necrophilia.
2. I've got an open sore in my throat.
3. My family is a bunch of pathological self-promoters stuck in some early childhood omnipotence phase. In the most extreme case, they might write a pop-culture essay on the issue of why the avant-garde belly dances DESPITE IT ALL, but that's about it.

You've made my shitlist
(L7)

I'm like, 'Excuse me? Could you maybe help me with the beef here, I don't know what kind of beef to buy.'
I'm standing in front of a large freezer at Lidl.

Cue heterosexual female communication designer in blue and grey striped cardigan.
'Pardon?'
'I'm supposed to buy beef for dinner, but they've got stewing beef and stir-fry beef, and I don't know what kind I need to get.'
'Well, sorry, but I don't actually know whether your mother needs stewing beef or stir-fry beef.'
'My mother's dead. She's been dead for ages.'
'And your father?'
'He's one of those assertive left-wing wankers with an above-average income permanently doing stuff with art, living between the galleries and boutiques on August-strasse. Every day up to eleven prostitutes, hair wax and highlighter pens to colour in melancholy expressionist artworks he puts together out of black-and-white record covers. And then at night he and his gallery owner nail them to the wall on LSD. His life's all about depressing music. The Melvins, Julie Driscoll, Neil Young – as if no

one else made music apart from Neil Young and Bob Dylan. Every week he orders records for three hundred dollars. I hardly know him.'

'So where do you live?'

'With my brother and sister.'

'And what do your brother and sister do for a living?'

'My sister's called Annika and she's a scheming marketing bitch. My brother Edmond designs motifs for a selection of textile items sold by a social commerce firm based in Leipzig. He uploads his designs on to an online platform and waits until someone has the ridiculous idea of walking around in a cream hoodie with "Our national colours are crap" printed on it in black, red and yellow. And he even designs T-shirts with the slogan "I'm not an alcoholic, I'm drunk – alcoholics go to meetings!" He's twenty-three, a mixture of Marlon Brando and, er, who else? I don't know. He owns one of only five hundred existing pairs of Pro Bowl 2007 Air Force 1 Nikes. Unemployed, demonstratively arrogant, Ray Davis fan.'

If found, please return to the club.

'And what about you?'

'Like any underage drug addict with an ability for reflection, my tendency to escape from reality expresses itself in a pronounced reading addiction. I devour everything from enlightened literature about Pakistani psychoanalysts to theses on the links between Moby Dick and Nazism. I shrug off daylight with a dismissive gesture.'

'Well, it was lovely talking to you!'

'Yeah, great, see you around!'

* * *

I remember the time when I did things in good weather other than pulling the blinds down. Dejected, I give myself a shot of legendary non-fiction on the praxis of DJ CULTURE:

Over the past twenty seconds the situation on the dancefloor has altered drastically. Cheers, screams, new levels of extremity everywhere out there.

'Hi, Edmond. When are you coming home?'

'Don't know. I'm hanging with Luther at the store on Alte Schönhauser. Penny should be here any minute, that girl with the PCP.'

'And when are you coming back?'

'I don't really know. Thingy and Kleini just came in, you know, the guy with the girlfriend who always wants her own way— Is it mixed by you? It's mixed like shit! Berlin is here to mix everything with everything, man!'

'Did you make that up?'

'Berlin is here to mix everything with everything, man? I steal from anywhere that resonates with inspiration or fuels my imagination, Mifti. Films, music, books, paintings, cold-cuts poetry, photos, conversations, dreams . . .'

'Street signs, clouds . . .'

'Light and shadows, that's right, because my work and my theft are authentic as long as something speaks directly to my soul. It's not where I take things from – it's where I take them to.'

'So you didn't make it up?'

'No. It's from some blogger.'

'But when are you coming home?'

'Hey, I don't know exactly, maybe soon.'

7

'When?'

'Soon. Maybe in a minute.'

'Huh?'

'Yeah, in a minute, right now.'

'OK, bye.'

I open our front door to the new housekeeper, the shock at all this excessive neglect spreading across her foolish face. She looks at me as if she was scared of coming across putrefying animal corpses inside the flat.

'Why do you want a housekeeper, Annika?'

'Because it's totally awesome to get your bedlinen ironed and all that.'

'But don't you think it's really bad having all those people in your possession?'

'You know, Mifti, you used to be just a poor little neglected kid and now you're such a poor little neglected rich kid you've forgotten that housekeepers are human beings.'

Frau Messerschmidt is retired and works cash-in-hand for twelve hours a day because her husband's a pathologically argumentative bastard who never leaves the house. The question arises as to whether I can deal with staff who talk about their family background and my truancy tendencies after only sixty minutes of self-sacrificing labour. I want staff who don't speak German and don't shoot melancholy glances in my direction showing me how terrible it all is, especially the thing with the ethnic-patterned dress that hasn't been ironed in two years, and that life just doesn't get any better later on. Ironing is a whole nother story. Daylight is a whole 'nother story.

Funnily enough, I know exactly what I want: not to grow up. In a couple of years I won't have the energy to think deep thoughts about what colour my first ever sofa cover ought to be. I'll look back sadly at a development process scarred by excessively counterproductive crashes 'n' burns and be mortally ashamed of what I'm currently hammering into the computer, in finest throwing-a-sprat-to-catch-a-mackerel style – I think that's what they call it. Because by then I'll presumably have finally made sense of Foucault, because I'll have different yardsticks and I'll have killed my family and I'll know suddenly that all this – this pile of trash collaged out of unstructured daily routines and truancy and sweat-soaked sheets – was the best time of my life.

Edmond comes home. He's brought cigarettes and three slabs of hash in an Aldi bag. He doesn't just look like Marlon Brando, he's compiled an important element of his life straight out of his biography – the minimalist interior decoration for our flat. Two rooms laid out with a total of thirteen mattresses, with free access for any and every unknown junkie off the street. Edmond thinks it's good to sleep in a different part of the flat every night, and in summer he always leaves the front door open so that the whole fresh air thing works better. So you could hardly call it breaking and entering; all a burglar would have to do is walk in through the open front door and put the nearest MacBook Pro or whatever under their jacket and stroll out again. One time Edmond unknowingly opened the entry door downstairs to burglars and all our neighbours got robbed. A speaker system, a cleverly placed overhead projector, ashtrays and throws printed with comic characters. A white poster on one unrendered wall, with minuscule letters saying, *Nowhere better than this place.*

Crap music is crap music; I just don't find it funny. 'Good Day' by The Kinks is pretty much OK, it starts with an alarm clock, then comes Patsy Cline, overrated, 'Sunday Morning' by Margo Guryan, the Violent Femmes singing 'Love is gone', and I can't help telling myself there must be a grain of truth in there somewhere, thinking of shredded body parts in the snow. They're primarily songs written in the pre-ecstasy era.

This is Edmond's iTunes library. I tell him I'm feeling magnificent. He tells me the song 'Hey Hey, My My' represents the missing link between alt-rock and punk, and that generally accepted standards define anyone as an absolute provincial hick if they use the words 'techno' and 'culture' to describe a youth movement that regards itself as alternative, rather than chav discos for the upper income bracket. Seeing ecstasy, techno and yourself as a combination to break down all boundaries is so nineties, he tells me, just like coke is so eighties and curly hair's the new straight hair.

'But that combination, as you call it, is all I've got left,' I say.

We lay the hash slabs out on the carpet in the hall and dilute it by spreading crumbled-up *Lebkuchen* evenly across the top and then ironing it in.

'Oh God, look, I've got this incredibly huge bump in my eye socket, I bet it's going to be a massive spot!' I say.

Edmond is brushing his teeth. As he answers, 'Maybe it'll be a boil,' a froth of toothpaste drips down the front of the monkey's head on his Christopher Kane T-shirt.

'You bastard!'

'Karl Marx had boils on his arse for years and then he got them lanced good and proper.'

'Are there any women who've made action movies? Apart from Karl Marx, I mean?'

'Angelina Jolie. *Lara Croft*.'

'Directors, you mong.'

'Oh right, no idea.'

'There aren't any, are there?'

'No, you're right, there aren't any. Maybe that's a job for you.'

'I'll just go out and revolutionize the female action movie genre.'

'The action melodrama, it'll be.'

'The female action melodrama.'

'The feminist action melodrama.'

'No, the anti-feminist action melodrama! Someone told me today I was scared of getting close to people. What's your take?'

'My take is, where Mifti comes from they eat our worst nightmares for breakfast. Wherever Mifti goes she leaves a trail of burnt-out hearts behind her. She's here today and gone tomorrow. But for most people she's the incarnation of the Sputnik crisis turned woman. I'll just treat you like shit.'

The day refuses to take a decisive turn. Let's talk about three-year-old Aeneas. Several hours ago he was hanging upside down from a climbing frame, shouting at one of his parents, 'No, I don't wanna go to yoga!'

My sister invited his mother to dinner at our place in her cream-coloured nylon coat, and to add insult to injury she brought him along too. Right now he's playing with a cannon made of Lego, which can catapult small tin soldiers right across the living room, and the whole world expects me to make him a knight's outfit out of

11

some weird insulation sheeting stuff. I'm the perfect image of chaos and disarray and paedophobia, and his mother interrupts me to say, 'Sorry, is the noise bothering you?'

'No – he's just a kid,' I answer.

We eat fish fingers. Aeneas is sitting on a shelf in his knight's outfit, waiting for something or other.

'What are you doing up there?' I ask.

No answer.

'Aeneas, where are you?'

'On a train.'

'And where are you going?'

'To Barcelona. To fight.'

'Oh Annika, you're the only person I know who can wear everything!'

'Thanks, that's really—'

'Seriously, you can wear absolutely anything.'

'Oh no, I'm just really careful about what I buy. That's probably why it looks like I can wear anything.'

'Yeah, you can wear just anything.'

Annika is what you'd call a cross between Germany's sex-shop pioneer and former stunt pilot Beate Uhse, Germaine Greer and Mother Teresa. She's worked her way up to a position where people now look up to her, she looks a million dollars and she adores Argentinian beef. The thing is, searching for some ancient traumatic odysseys through the Berlin underground scene clad in neon T-shirts is pretty much out, in her book. Aeneas's father has come round as well. He's sitting slap bang across from me, out of his depth without the slightest idea of how to maintain a semblance of family life for the sake of this socially disturbed child. It's a family life that was shipwrecked on the rocks of his lack of intelligence and his ex-wife's effusive emancipation ambitions. She's just talking about how her new lover bought a set of glass carafes for four hundred euros on eBay.

They used to take baths at our place in the dim and distant past, when they had the builders in. We could always hear them through the crack of the door, arguing in a pseudo overwrought way about feminism and the feminist alliance with patriarchal society and female sexuality restructured by men through the whole pornography thing until it's not sexuality at all. And how the womb is only a product of discourse and all that. And it was great because neither of them could get out of the bath to get a bit of distance on the subject – they didn't want to walk around naked in our flat.

Terrible lives are the best stroke of luck.

When he notices me noticing him he gives a sudden croak: 'Hey, Mifti, were you also at Luther's store on Schönhauser today? They had some dumb sit-down rave.'

'Oh, yeah. No, what makes you think that? Edmond was there on his own. I don't even know what you mean by a sit-down rave.'

'What?'

'What d'you mean?'

'Must be the time zones. You look like you've got mini jet lag, and all the writing on the cigarettes is in English.'

'Sorry?'

'The cigarettes, where did you get them?'

'Edmond just brought them home.'

'Oh right, cool. I didn't smoke when I was your age. I was still learning to tie knots in balloons.'

'When I was your age . . . ha ha ha.'

'Ha ha ha ha ha!'

It makes me want to puke, all that adult blustering and filibustering, all that talk about how little Aeneas pointed at someone at the next table in a restaurant and now his dumb mother had to go and say that stupid German saying beloved of all grown-ups, 'Aeneas, we don't point naked fingers at people with clothes on!' And Aeneas went and poked his finger in a potato and carried on pointing it and the potato at the woman regardless. Zero punchline, but still, 'Ha ha ha ha ha ha ha!'

Annika's mobile rings. Frau Pegler has informed my father that I haven't been to school for the past six weeks. I don't give a fuck, really I don't.

'You're not the victim, you're the sole perpetrator.'

'Excuse me, but your thing's burning!'

'School qualifications? What do I need them for? I've got a bike and I can keep myself entertained just as well with French films where all the protagonists stuff some kind of crap into themselves out of handmade clay pots while cheating on their wives.'

20:13. Text message from Father in Tel Aviv: 'What R U going to do now?'

20:29. Promising text message to Father in Tel Aviv: 'Return to petty criminality no longer an option.'

20:33. 'Y don't you call?'

20:34. Text to Ophelia in her androgynous phase: 'Know what, I want to shower you with love right now. Everything. Anytime.'

Foreword

I grew up wild and I want to stay wild. It's 3 a.m. and
my partied-out body is sitting in a taxi, submerged to
death in its role as a victim. The driver's telling me about
his son, who's left his wife after ten years, and about his
own wife, who's cheating on him, and about God, with
whom he claims to have a pretty good connection. That's
why he's willing to forgive homos, because it's like not
their fault they're that way. I'm running a fever,
coordination problems, a BAC of 0.1 per cent and I've
gone and agreed to go to a place of absolute opportun-
istic inhibition all over again. It's all about my respect-
worthiness, about steel and concrete, about a huge
glazed façade that can be closed up using mobile
shutters, about my fear of death, it's about the explosion
of perception and perhaps also a little bit about an
organized form of aural events.

My wildness is a characteristic idiosyncrasy. I can either
do what I want and satisfy my characteristics or just not.

Doing what I want is dangerous because it really
makes me vulnerable. Not doing it is not an option.

That's why I lie to you. I say, it's primarily a matter of
principle right now.

I'm sixteen years old and presently capable of nothing but wanting to establish myself – despite colossal exhaustion – in contexts that have nothing to do with the society in which I go to school and suffer from depression. I'm in Berlin.

It's all about my delusions.

I can't believe I'm exposing myself to all this crap all over again, on cognac-coloured four-inch heels. An industrial wasteland, of course; from far off you can see a former power plant in which the plan is to forget myself in half an hour at the most. I negotiate a path fenced in with neon tubes, generally regarded as the most awesome path in the world, which has never interested me, for some unfathomable reason. I find my dissociative identity disorder more interesting than anything this city constantly spews in my face. Facing a ten-foot security chief called Syd, I pretend to be on the guest list of a barman who spends his daylight hours attempting to represent the confusing prospects of our urban world by means of contemporary charcoal sketches. I circumnavigate a mile-long queue of overstyled 23-year-olds from stable family backgrounds, in whose eyes I'm not a human being but merely underdressed and fickle. Oral incontinence. They're chucking shit in my face. I'm a motherfucking immoral cunt and I need to get a handle on my life.

The big question of the night: 'Hey, what's goin' down here?'

The big answer of the night: 'Hey, nuttin's goin' down.'

The big outcome of the night: 'Wicked, no queue, taxi's waiting back there, World Health Organization definitions everywhere you look, Jesus.'

From where I stand in front of the DJ console, on the left behind a big glass wall is a long bar, and there's various seating options; on the right behind the dance floor is one of the unmissable darkrooms. As far as the eye can see, these pseudo-ravished individuals in their mid-twenties are trying to dance their souls out of their bodies. I'm sitting on leather upholstery, unimpressed by some absurd music style, being asked the most important question of the night after only ten minutes of unspectacular exuberance crap. Sixty-foot ceilings, two thousand five hundred people and HIV-positive Ophelia, who I've arranged to meet at the entrance. She looks gorgeous and anorexic in equal parts, wearing a half-open bomber jacket with nothing underneath, teamed with black leggings and satin Lanvin sandals with mirrored heels, and I talk undiluted crap the minute I see her.

'Everything's fine as long as some simple silhouette is transformed into an absolute must-have this season, huh, honey? Classic elegance.'

'I'd step into any breach for you anytime, Mifti.'

'And the ruffled fall of a silk curtain conceals most of your body.'

'I really want to have a good time.'

'But it's just too hot in here.'

So then at some point she asks with a gesture towards the ladies, 'See that guy over there?'

It's the guy whose presence has prevented me from running past him nonchalantly to the cigarette machine. Just for a change, he doesn't awaken any sexual yearning – only a bit of an emotional affection attack because he's so cute, because he's toned and he looks so totally washed, in contrast to all the chubbed-out chauvinist hippies around here. I'm only talking uninspired crap anyway.

Ophelia says, 'He's got ecstasy.'

I walk towards him, ignoring the fact that she's waiting for a witty response.

'Could you possibly sort us out with two units?'

'Ummm . . .'

'Since when have we been good friends?'

'Ummm?'

'Take a quick look at the heels on my friend's weave-look shoes. Pretty reflective, huh?'

'So you're interested in fashion as well, are you?'

'Do I look like I am?'

'That coat alone, it's really – and the belt with it. Do they go together?'

'No.'

'So you mix 'n' matched.'

'Yeah, well, no. I like it when men do it, when they wear suits and that. Like those disgraced English ministers, that's kind of sexy.'

The guy looks at my torn polyester skirt and expects two fivers from me. I take money out of my shoe, coming across as a mix of mentally disturbed and nervously excited. He gives me the pills more inconspicuously than absolutely necessary, looking me up and down like the world's thinnest-skinned person.

I ask, 'Are you up for oral sex?'

He answers, 'How old are you? Sixty-three?'

And with that he releases me into a never-ending well of sadness.

Ophelia is extremely attractive – a phlegmatic action heroine. Whenever I go looking for Ophelia, I always find her sitting in front of a full-length mirror with a razor blade, a complete wreck. Whenever she hasn't

18

consumed any drugs for more than six hours she ends up with an attack of hysteria that wants to kill her, and tries to rid herself of her facial muscles. We met because she occasionally temps in school canteens, out of some half-hearted need to get close to reality despite being in the top tax bracket.

'I'd like the creamed polenta with spinach and can I have pasta out of the other pan instead of potatoes, please?'

Her: 'What other pan?'

Me: 'The second or third from the left over there.'

'Just pointing would've done the trick.'

'And pudding?'

'You've already had your dessert.'

'I've definitely not had my dessert, I've only just come in here because I had social science on the third floor.'

'Never mind your motherfucking social sciences, you still just took a pudding, baby!'

'No I didn't!'

'I can't just run around here chucking forty portions of custard into teenage faces that nobody's paid for. What am I supposed to call you now? Impotent wanker?'

'What on earth are you talking about?'

'Shut your fucking mouth, you smart arse.'

'Get up, you cunt, and bow.'

'Pardon?'

'GET UP YOU CUNT AND BOW!'

Ophelia threw a large ladleful of buckwheat bake at me. I chucked my classmate Olivia Stüter's custard at her, she emptied a portion of spinach intended for two hundred thirteen- to sixteen-year-olds over my head. While the two of us maintained strict eye contact all along. We conjured up a channel between us, through which we managed to stare at each other as if we were head over heels in love.

She informed me that she was the perfect mirror for my true yearnings. And I just swallowed it, dialled her phone number, listened to her saying I urgently had to throw away a number of items of clothing she didn't like, and answered that she was a dead woman.

'If there's one thing you can count on in this world, it's being mentally and physically violated.'

It may all sound pretty implausible, but that's just the way it was back then.

From: Ophelia
To: Mifti
Subject: Go Fuck Yourself
Date: Sun, 4 November 2007, 22:12

I have to tell you my dream. You'll like it. We wanted to get together and I was supposed to visit you at your place. A huge old apartment building. Mirrored stairwell. Twenty doors per floor. I've even done a drawing of it, shame I can't scan it in. I went up the stairs. There were dogs fighting over the remains of a donkey. It was quite dark because there was only one window in the entire hallway. In a corner was a table and chairs. I looked around and realized that this vestibule covered in vulture-shit was part of your flatshare.

I was curious because there was an unlocked door. The gap between the door and the frame was really wide and I could see it wasn't locked. I opened it and looked into a little room with a metal bed inside, and on it was an old man covered in zillions of pus-filled wounds. He heard me and moved. I left the room. A girl came out of a double door. I didn't quite know if it was you but she looked like you, and she went to the washbasin and washed her hands. I didn't dare ask who she was because I'd forgotten your name. I couldn't remember if it was Ute or Uta. At some point I asked if she was Mifti. She said in an unfriendly way, no, she's inside.

It was your flatmate. Her name was Claudia.

We went into the bathroom, and there was a crowd of people in flipflops made of old car tyres, all in just as bad a state as the guy on the bed. You'd invited all these people round and I thought, she really is disturbed! They were all vying for your attention. Two women even got in the bathtub naked to impress you. All the others, there were at least seven of them, stood around the bath. I just carried on walking without saying a word to you. And you looked totally out of your depth. In the next room, which was incredibly large, there was an orgy going on. A man got down on all fours in front of me and pushed his arse out so I could fuck him. And I suddenly had a cardboard dick but it was only two-dimensional, just like the condom I wanted to put on it. And of course that didn't work. The End.

From: Mifti
To: Ophelia
Subject: RE: Go Fuck Yourself
Date: Mon, 5 November 2007, 00:12

And how do you interpret all that?

In my last dream I flew to the Amazon in an inflatable plastic helicopter. After a while we had to make an emergency landing in the rainforest in the dusk and my brother said, 'You can decide now whether to get dressed or not.'

Then someone shouted: 'Oh, a melody in the night!' and we saw a huge, vacant hotel with a pool and a squash court. All the passengers spent their time lying around blind drunk on car roofs discussing tropane alkaloids. Alice was there too. She wasn't human. She adjusted her face, stroked the back of my hand tenderly and reminded me what she and I really are – real-life individuals or whatever you call it, in a real-life society, with real-life desires that can't just be sliced out of our real-life heads. You were lying under this big palm tree and waving at me the whole time. I went up to you, so utterly upset I couldn't even speak any more, and you whispered, 'Mifti, you're in a strange land, you're acting like you've just got off the ark and of course you're much too thin-skinned.'

From: Ophelia
To: Mifti
Subject: Go Fuck Yourself
Date: Mon, 5 November 2007, 06:28

The fact that I couldn't remember your real name in my dream shows up my superficiality. I don't listen properly. The fact that you'd invited so many people or women at the same time is down to my subjective perception of what kind of person you are. I seem to think you're someone who wants to arouse attention by going to extremes, who's egocentric and hurls their problems or innermost thoughts in people's faces for the sake of short-term liberation, and enjoys and needs their reactions. An absolute perpetrator but a victim too, who I end up fucking. Funny, isn't it? And I don't even know you well enough. Last night I met you at an awards ceremony. You had your black velour jacket on and you went over to the lift when you saw me. I screamed, 'Mifti, I hate you!' You screamed, 'But why?' I screamed, 'For you with your 24× zoom lens on Alice, any kind of love based on mutual affection is too much to ask! Why can't other people ever enter your fucking field of vision?'

I started doing nothing else in maths lessons but developing the next dream to be described in spectacular detail. I failed to develop an understanding of binomial equations or the fact that you can give names to angles in trigonometric functions. All I developed was an all-encompassing love of adjectives.

From: Ophelia
To: Mifti
Subject: RE: No subject
Date: Sat, 19 January 2008, 10:28

Is it possible that everything's just chemistry or biology? Then wouldn't the point of falling in love be only reproduction? So why do I only ever fall in love with women? But still want brutal sex with men? I keep reading this book about serial killers and I think it's altered my sexuality. It describes everything, and there are things I'd never even imagined in all my life. Ninety per cent of murders are about sex. I think all wars are about sex. It's a pretty selfish act somehow, the whole shagging thing. You want to be desired; you want to give the other person pleasure because what you can do for them gives you pleasure. You want to be sexy or for the other person to like you. You want an orgasm. Sometimes when I sleep with someone the sounds we make aren't real, maybe. But maybe they are. Do we exaggerate? I think the whole animal urge thing at the beginning (when I don't generally reflect on things) is only there to tie you to each other. Nature probably did that on purpose. Then I can do stuff legally that I'd usually only do on my own. Once I loved someone, with my every pore and dripping with kitsch, and I just switched off my brain. What a relief. Because it wasn't just a reflex, it was suddenly imploding and going soft. So soft that all I could do was smile, because I couldn't feel anything apart from myself melting away. And from then on it wasn't an animal urge any more, it was divine and sexy. You ought to stop surrendering yourself to truck drivers and only let someone you love bite your neck, because with everyone else you're probably really some kind of animal. You are anyway. And none of it matters.

So I'm climbing some steel staircase side by side with Ophelia. Meanwhile she's discreetly getting off on the fact of her patented existence as a photographer with her own vision and ideas and all that black and white crap. She always says she doesn't see colours any more now that she's so sick. She's just gone colour blind. I read this interview with David LaChapelle once and sussed out that the colour blindness story is lifted from him. When you ask her where she gets her inspiration, things usually get abstract. The African steppe, cold snakes of the air and Jil Sander suits reflected in the parquet with cheeseburger telephones, with a stuffed toy jackal emerging from them covered in pig's blood or whatever. So she's an artist, right? And she hates dull people who stop her on the street and bother her. What's worse than wealth are these hypocritical proto-artists who claim to be absolute scum and make fun of all the heirlooms I possess. Silk napkins, necklaces, not even silver cutlery, just two silver spoons. Not one critic understands what it means to shove your own deservingness in people's yellowed faces day after day, for money, because you need a bit of money for a change, plain and simple. 'Their problem, these critics' problem,' she always says, 'isn't even their arrogance, being arrogant is aristocratic and all that. The worst thing is their stupidity, or not even their stupidity, the worst thing is their laziness. You make a statement and it's neutralized and watered down by, like, I don't know, pathologizing it or psychologizing it or marking it down as unintentional, out of pure laziness. But the whole anarchy thing isn't a mistake, it's meant to be exactly that way, d'you know what I mean?'

On principle, we only ever walk side by side when we're not obliged to talk to each other.

We share cocktails and it's a fantastic moment, I don't even know why. I suddenly feel showered with the love I mentioned a few hours ago in my text to her. Two hysterical shadows wave at us from a concrete couch, and I take their presence as a threat. Ophelia introduces an over-fifty-year-old hardcore restaurateur with above-average income as her most down-to-earth friend. I repeat: concrete couch. He says hello. He has a banana stain on his black shirt and brightly coloured trainers and a twenty-year-old girl on his arm called Samantha, who's either mentally retarded or out for a fur coat.

'Whatever you do, don't tell Miss Sixth-Former over there that the guy she's here with looks like he'll lose his entire restaurant empire in a round of poker. OK, Mifti?'

'Huh?'

'They're getting married in four weeks, Jesus, and Albrecht's gambling everything she loves him for every night without even looking at his cards first. At one of those gambling clubs run by a trannie in a claw necklace on Schiffbauerdamm. Blind All In, that's what they call it. That skull over there's the engagement ring, by the way.'

Inevitably, I get left out and end up following the two and a half über-established freaking icons obligingly into the private smokers' room, overly sensitive and unbalanced.

Samantha dumps her genuine pale-blue calfskin Hermès bag on me, adjusts her Margiela cardigan and changes her Acne jeans for a flannel miniskirt from Marc Jacobs – and Ophelia whispers in my ear, 'How can anyone be such an uninspired dresser?'

Then we all start exchanging pleasantries about the falafel wrap that Ophelia puked up on the kitchen floor a couple of hours ago, and pop our pills casually but in unison. Albrecht offers us two lines of ketamine, which is used by vets as an anaesthetic and has a hallucinogenic effect in small doses. He says, 'You know what you can tell your friends at school, Mifti? That ketamine entails the complete dissolution of your own existence, four years in a coma and the worst brain spiralling, but apart from that it gets you DANCING like a maniac, non-stop, no matter who or where you are.'

Samantha says, 'I just can't fucking believe how incredibly dumb you all are! We're talking about an anaesthetic drug, and as you might imagine it can anaesthetize you! And when you're anaesthetized you stop breathing. And when you stop breathing you run out of oxygen at some point. And that's not good.'

The stuff stings like fuck in your nose.

And this is my life.

It displays a fine crystalline structure, is transparent in

colour and its consistency varies greatly with temperature. It's blurred, it's an underwater tank from which you have to escape as quickly as possible and suddenly you're swimming through a swarm of oversized dangerous fish at five hundred metres below sea level. I decide to erase every moment of clarity with ketamine or the words 'Fifty whisky and sodas please!' from now on. Interim worlds are my only relation to reality. I almost want to say the truth, oh God, and after years frozen like a rabbit in the headlights, now I'm reaching out and grabbing life by the balls. I can't see anything but dark blue waves, seaweed and ochre sperm whales with their jaws wide open. Whenever I'm just about to end up between the gums of one of these sperm whales and therefore suddenly absolutely convinced I'll be dead in a matter of seconds, the world blacks out for a moment. I don't know whether I'm lying down or standing up or still sitting on the lap of some long-haired fucked-up bum who's fallen asleep with a bare torso in one of the sofa niches designed for casual sex. The first thing I see is a threatening number of black silhouettes. After that an overweight woman in a full-body latex suit comes towards me, taking three more or less sexless individuals for walkies around the premises on leashes, and tries to hand me a napkin.

I ask her, 'Could you perhaps pass me the boa constrictor for a moment?' My view is obscured by an open sore in the fish's throat as I swim into its mouth. I close my eyes, open them again and find myself in a rectangular toilet cubicle with Ophelia and two men. As soon as I become conscious of my body and the fact that I'm capable of independent thought, my short-term and long-term memory are suddenly out of sync. The past and present merge into one, the predatory fish gullet and my hysterical surroundings fade into each other, my perception of time is transformed into a huge field of piled-up memories. It's a near-death experience, I start to panic, then I persuade myself that this state has nothing to do with my imminent death but with neurochemical processes in the temporal lobes of my brain. Ophelia's standing on the toilet lid so that she can cut three lines of speed on the dividing wall between the toilets. Laughing, she throws first her belt and then one of her shoes over the cubicle door. I can no longer distinguish the basslines coming out of Europe's best sound system from the people banging on the door from the outside; I just can't help monging out in my usual abstruse dancing style in the tiny space, finding out all over again under tortuous circumstances what the best beat is for dislocating your left shoulder. I have my own hands, my own legs and my own sense of balance. I fight my way through walls of steel and the over-dimensioned neutrality of a situation one could objectively categorize as 'inappropriate'. As I said, steel. Puddles of vodka, body parts, mouths, hair, sweat, moles in armpits, a German hunt terrier tattooed on the upper arm of a girly PR trainee, raw flesh and strobes.

'Jesus, look at the size of your pupils!'

'Yeah, thanks for the conversation.'

The ecstasy guy from before is now wearing a blue sweatshirt, chewing gum and pressing me against the wall like in a soft-rock video.

I shout, 'Hey, maa-an, get off me please!'

'Can I take a photo of them?'

'Kindly fuck right off!'

'Just let me take a picture of your pupils, OK?'

'No, go away, go away!'

'Don't you know that film, *Romance*? You only love me when there's a table between us.'

'I know *Last Tango in Paris*, where the girl shoots Marlon Brando out of nowhere, and then he like sticks his chewing gum under the balcony railing, just before he dies with a huge hole in his stomach. Yes, yes, yes.'

'How do you like the music?'

'I love this club but I don't love Berlin!'

'Right answer!'

'Do you always talk in platitudes when you're embarrassed?'

'Yeah.'

He has stubby eyelashes and he stares me triumphantly in the face. His eyes shine as if they were looking into a pond reflecting every available light source in Berlin at the same time. Something's swelling up there that only he can see, a different world. Keen to wipe the circumstances off the face of the earth, I try to stop my body from ending up between the gums of the person standing opposite me. Two thousand five hundred people have taken whizz to stay awake tonight and narcotics to fly away.

At 8:26 a.m., Ophelia is simultaneously bored to death and glad to have found me asleep but unharmed at the back end of one of the bars. She asks me in all seriousness if I want to have a sitdown for a minute. Get down on your knees, sweetheart, and kiss the ground. There's no talking on the leather upholstery of her choice; instead we look past each other seriously and stylishly and act as if communication might work magnificently via an unbounded tolerance of each other's silence.

'Shall we go? It's so dull here.'

29

'Yeah.'

'What were you wearing, actually, the first time you kissed Alice?'

I only manage the twenty-four-day march home by imagining getting shot at every step.

Mother
(Pink Floyd)

Of course it was a huge catastrophe when you looked across the road out of the front window in your pissed pants and died three hours later. Your system collapsed from internal bleeding and took on a life of its own, and your unmade-up eyes practically screamed at me in the overcrowded emergency room, telling me you knew I was going through hell because you refused to speak to me. You knew I'd slit all my veins the moment you stopped talking to me, I tried it regularly with a razor blade as a kid to make it somehow clear to you how terrible you were. And suddenly you were suspicious of life. The final falling of all chains, the death criteria. You possess me, you dominate me, I have nothing to do with you. The entire world despises me. It's possible that I murdered you under more civilized circumstances. Men want to rape me, of course, certain parts of my body are constantly swollen, this world is paradise, pain doesn't exist. You just have to believe it for long enough. You were brain dead in one of those hospital nightgowns out of an early-evening TV show, and I was obliged to switch off a machine which would have prevented your heart from stopping. Hate, cream-coloured polyester shirts with holes for the thumbs, traditionally relaxed conversations about volleyball teams and sea-salt face masks, I mean . . .

Listen, Mother, your spewed-up shit will have my entire approval my whole life long . . .

I was driven to extremes by a masochist machine within. Since you died, no unsuspected violence has lurked behind the doors of the places I live any more – just unbounded disappointment. I saw dead robin embryos on the metal staircase to our flat, fallen out of their nest and crushed beneath your feet. I learned to light matches, I weaned myself off my inborn trust and found myself forced to start idolizing you and all the fibres of meat drawn out between your teeth. If you hadn't died I'd still be lying shocked to death in a pool of parental blood, puke and vaginal secretions. I entirely failed to savour all the advantages associated with your death, burning the money in the condolence letters and not speaking because I thought it would come across as more authentic somehow if I sat around with my pale skin emphasizing the impression of pensiveness. BIG MISTAKE. I suffered exclusively. So now this letter is my weapon of expression against the fear of not surviving it all. I lay down in front of some wallpapered radiator and just waited for everything to stop.

I want vision. If I do everything I can to steer my desires and dreams and characteristics in a com-pletely different direction so I don't have to leave you, am I turning away from all that's dearest and deepest: vision? Or are things like vision necessity working itself out? Oh God, I don't want to write all this stuff any more. The other day I watched all Gena Rowlands's movies. I have to say you were a mixture of Gena Rowlands and all the roles she played in John Cassavetes's films.

Gena Rowlands as *A Woman Under the Influence*, plunging into a deep crisis in the intensely acted family drama.

Gena Rowlands in *Opening Night* as a Broadway actress who plunges into a deep crisis.

Gena Rowlands in *Gloria* as a courageous woman who takes on gangsters to protect a little boy, and that kind of plunges her into a deep crisis at some point.

You even had two 9-mm semi-automatic pistols and thought you were a mafia boss wanted in twenty-eight countries. Jesus, I just remembered that this minute. And that the whole thing between us was a love between two adults with equal rights, living in a hideout for female terrorists under difficult circumstances and realizing every morning that they've never seen each other before in their lives. A pretty sexual love based on reciprocity and mutual consent. Of course I've since been driven to extremes by a sadistic machine within. I ran away to be fully reflected and balanced in this terrible city until the end of my days. Now I want to blow every establishment I enter into smithereens in a sponta- neous suicide bombing. Didn't I tell you once that I'd help you to destroy me? I'm old enough now to want to know everything about your past and to see that I have more to do with your life before I was born than any of the people who were part of it.

You know you're the only one I love.

Mifti

PS: And I know you only did what was best for me.

Right now I'm lying on red cord mats next to something not quite substantial, puked into a pale yellow toilet bowl, and I've been skinned. Above me hangs my now blood-soaked T-shirt. Someone's torn it off me and then applied a specially manufactured knife to my coccyx to make the first cut along my backbone. Then the skin was separated from the flesh. The scalp at the back is the easiest to remove. The face is left, a few scraps of skin on the knuckles too. Hands and feet dangle because they've been severed at the joints.

I'm nothing but one huge wound and I'm dissolving into my surroundings. So this glorified freaking youth is written on my skin, on the upper-class skin of which I consist, of which I primarily consisted before Alice, who is revealed ever more clearly in the contours of the interior fittings wavering in all directions, and now stands suddenly before me.

She's been through excessive plastic surgery. With my authentic martyr's gaze, I estimate the ratio of her hips to her arse and the tension of her muscles under the whole excessive Chinese silk dress thing she's got going on. My circulation is set to collapse forever within the next ten minutes due to the high blood loss; she knows it, I know it, and in the best case God knows it too.

'Your eyes, Mifti, I've never seen such a state of mind. So relaxed. I don't think you're picking up on what's going on around you any more. But you're still . . . yes, you really are still alive.'

I scream, 'Do you even know what you've done?'

'You're blind, do you understand? If you'd got old you'd have looked back at some point and realized that the entire memory of your whole happy youth consists only of me. Of the hope that I'd play you *I need you* again in a mega-disco flooded with something transcendental. And then you'd have told yourself I never even existed. I was only some inappropriate fucked-up individual through whom you had to learn that devotion can lead to loss of self, and this loss of self has nothing to do with love any more, only with auto-aggression. Can you tell how you're transcending right now?'

'I hate you.'

'You're a victim, just like all the others. It's so easy to create a victim out of someone. All they did was lock you in a dark room, and your suffering began, your agonies were intensified methodically and, cold as ice, you went through various stages of consciousness, and after a while it's perfectly natural for an all-encompassing trauma to develop in such an awful situation. The tiniest touch makes you perceive things that only exist in your imagination. What do you see? Insects, cockroaches, beetles crawling all over your body?'

'Erm.'

'You'd rather chop off your own arm than put up with it, wouldn't you?'

'Do you know who you look like right now, Alice?'

'This planet is made in such a way that there's only room left for victims. People have forgotten how to suffer.'

'Like Dorothy in *The Wizard of Oz* when she says, "Toto, I've a feeling we're not in Kansas any more."'

* * *

You know, I just want to apologize to myself for the fact that all the promises I made to my later self have just been ripped to shreds by some numb wind. That's why I started this whole diary crap in the first place. To be honest I think I'm trying to prove something to myself.

Success is like a timid deer, everything has to be just right: the stars, the . . . Oh, I don't know.
(Franz Beckenbauer)

Annika asks, 'How old is Ophelia anyway?'

'Twenty-eight.'

'Woah, OK. But she's still, like, "Hey, let's go out raving!"'

'Yeah, totally.'

22:35. Text from Ophelia in a state of total instability: 'I feel so harried right now, no time to relax. It distracts me so much from myself that I don't even feel time passing and everything just rushes past me in a totally over-powering way. As if I was standing at the side of a motorway and can't cross over. And I can't go back either, because of course I'm standing on the central reservation. A little accident to throw the world out of kilter wouldn't be bad right now.'

23:23. 'I've just realized that "totally overpowering" is one of your phrases. I almost never use it. You do, though. I'll just come round to see you.'

When Ophelia enters our flat with a spaghetti-topped pizza, Annika eyes her like someone who's superior to me, with her pearly-smooth skin, her elegance, her perfect hair.

Despite last night it's no longer all about me, but mainly about the hopeless situation I've got myself into. Something pretty grave has got bottled up inside my body, a mixture of proteolytic watery solutions and allocations of guilt. Quite a lot has gone off the rails. I see streets that want to eat me alive, stuffed penguins talk to me, saying things like, 'But animal testing's terrible too!' My surroundings are literally beginning to crack.

I'm lying next to Ophelia on a mattress squashed on to the balcony, a MacBook Pro resting on my raised legs just for a change.

The way you always tag 'so to speak' on to the end of your sentences, in fact the whole trick of making intellectual sentences confusing and breathless with those little filler words – impressive, Mifti!

We watch television clips about Belgian penguin freaks and a trailer for a film in which an eight-year-old boy gets fucked up the arse so incredibly overpoweringly that he has to go to hospital.

'Oh, Jesus, it sounds really bad, right, but that really turns me on.'

Whereupon of course I nod, totally head-fucked, and of course I ask, 'How d'you mean?'

'It's just like that disgusting sex scene with the fat-arse trucker in that awful film *Butterfly Kiss*. That's one of my top twenty masturbation turn-ons, I swear.'

Then we snog out of pure boredom.

'We're both so gender-confused, honey.'

* * *

'She just plays around so badly, you have absolutely no idea how much she hurts me. I don't know if it'd be any different if she knew about my mother.'

'It's still sick though.'

'That I love her? Yeah, sure.'

'Or not really sick, more like a displacement activity.'

'It's such torture.'

'In any case, you can't be anything but friends if you tell her the thing about your mother – if Alice still has a healthy cell in her body, sorry. And I don't know if she's capable of dealing with it.'

'What d'you mean?'

'Wouldn't it be better if you were just friends? No, it wouldn't be better. Wouldn't it be better if you never saw each other again?'

'Ophelia!'

'There's this phantasm, it was a real place in the Middle Ages, where fulfilled love was allowed to take place. A place for the experience that people are entitled to. I used to be in love with the boy in *The Never-Ending Story*, shit, what was his name again?'

'Atreyu.'

'Yeah, and I'd still say that boy was my greatest ever boyfriend. Of course I don't know him, and he doesn't know me.'

'Are you trying to reduce the whole thing to some teenage experience?'

'No, I'm just giving it as an example to make the whole thing a bit less abstract. Anyway, there was a place in my imagination where I could meet up with the boy. The things he does and his sense of humour mean he plays a pretty major role in my life. The idea I had of him kind of socialized me, I think. At least more than all the other

39

people I really hung out with at that time. It's a love
story, but the way the rest of the world sees it, I have to
have slept with him for it to be really acknowledged as
love. Maybe that's the problem. You know her so well.
And your whole bond only came out of the way you
came together, you only function together – now I think
we're getting to one of those overvalued spiritual kinship
points.'

'We only function together, hallelujah.'

'Yeah, man.'

'I don't know. I don't understand it.'

'Let's talk about sex.'

'It was so perfect.'

'Oh yeah?'

'Everything fitted perfectly, right from the beginning.
That week in her apartment and then after that all that
stuff in France with the sea and that, I mean normally
you're embarrassed or you say, oh, hold on a moment, I
think my leg's kind of trapped, or you get cramp or
whatever, because it never goes completely smoothly, but
in this case it just did. Go smoothly.'

'And . . .'

'I still want it to stay the way it is right now. And I'm
not jealous of her boyfriend or her forty lovers or
anything, I really like them all. I'd be jealous if she was
wading through the whole shit with some kind of pet.
With something that's cuter than me. If she was pregnant
I'd probably shoot myself outside her front door or
something.'

'She's forty-six, you're sixteen – you had sex when you
were fifteen. Or fourteen? And then you tell her you
recognize your dead mother in her. Something must have
got going inside her.'

'Like what?'

'Jesus, I don't know, scruples or whatever.'

'Can you please just give me a specific tip?'

'But Mifti, you know everything already, and there's no point anyway because you're in love and irrational.'

I treat myself to twenty minutes' contemplation before I expose myself to Annika's aggression.

We're sitting in the heavily frequented outdoor area of some former kindergarten converted into a hip location and have just decided to have a serious discussion about the problems arising from our new family structure. The European Cup is being projected live onto a 3 × 4 metre screen, and the atmosphere is one of totally tortured lack of inhibition. All the after-hours walking wounded are sitting at beer tent tables, slightly depressed, nodding their heads in reassurance now and then and eating pork chops to assuage the burnt-out wastelands wreaked by alcohol on twenty thousand stomachs. Twenty thousand stomachs full of burnt-out wasteland. I go inside to ask why nobody's coming to take our order. The waitress says, 'You see, the problem is, that's a summer awning out the front, and it wouldn't stand up to an unexpected rainstorm so we'll be putting it down within the next ten minutes, so the outside service will be restricted and, well, maybe you could just sit down inside, yeah?'

My life, my lack of discipline, my pet sheep, my tendency for auto-aggression, my self-doubts, my fear of not facing a tough test in time or a tough decision, and of course the fear of never having to get out of bed again, except to get hold of cigarettes every now and then and

41

then dump a dole application in the post box in a couple of years' time. My auto-aggression goes beyond a cluster of scars on my non-dominant lower arm; I've been intravenously injecting harmful substances and am now at risk of an unintentional fatal injury.

Everything goes on. It's not worth waiting for a life-changing event.

I'm an abused teenager. My sister, an empathetic interpreter, readily recognizes in me a deeply traumatized, hyper-intelligent person who has strayed from the right path and is sending out the famed silent cries for love/help from the brink of the abyss. I, on the other hand, am pretty pleased at my perfectly displayed attitude of arrogant, abused arsehole of a kid that flirts with its snobbish fucked-up status, unmasking the whole fucked-up status of its entire surroundings in one fell swoop. And as Annika is perfectly aware that she's part of the surroundings I've categorized as degenerated, this evening will presumably push her off a cliff into the depths of desperation. Basically, I'm spewing my guts on her designer shoes, but that's certainly way more interesting and exciting than many an artfully imagined intellectual outpouring. They've imbued me with a language that is not my own. That language is very lively, although certain words are put to extreme overuse. To carry off the smooth aloofness convincingly through all the insanity going on, it's important for the text to be flawless and perfectly structured. All in all, what remains to be said about me is this:

This young woman plays smoothly on elemental spinets like a gazelle with a bazooka.

* * *

I take a proper look at Annika for the first time in my life, registering the fact that her hair is black and she has large-scale white tattoos across her thin, pale upper arms, which you initially think must be a pigmentation disorder and then find original. She scratches, she squints to break your heart, and she acts as if the reason she's disappointed in me is a murder I'd committed of a family member. With the skeleton buried in the woods and a blood-soaked carpet ripped out of the flat and all that. Edmond has been in bed for fourteen hours now.

Last night he ran down Kastanienallee stark naked under the influence of the dissociative drug phency-clidine, and when he got home he started talking about a guy who cut off his dick on PCP, swallowed it and then regurgitated it later, laughing all the time. I love my brother and sister.

Last night I discussed the Ebo Hill film *Way Down* over tuna carpaccio and lemongrass vodka. Jürgen is pretty soulless and has insane guest-list capacities. We met at one of Ophelia's theme parties, and unlike many of the other guests he didn't want to take his pants off, and I thought that was great. At some point I'm, like, 'So, what do you do for a living?'

'I'm a student. But I'm a friend of Julianne Moore's. That makes it pretty difficult to take all the media studies lecturers seriously, with their receding hairlines.'

After that night I wrote on all my T-shirts in permanent marker: I SEE THE WORLD IN TWO DIMENSIONS.

Reality level two: I'm sitting at a table with this guy Jürgen. I'm an abused teenager. He and his whole fucked-up status as an aristocratic porn actor make me look pretty damn scheduled and scheming. One hundred and twenty-five established personalities are eating monkfish in pork nets and chatting about emotional low points that Asian actresses in art-house thrillers with international casts fail to capture. Wealthy construction moguls certainly don't frequent this establishment, because you don't get value for money. I jump out of a huge birthday cake wearing nothing but a feather headdress. Jürgen apologizes profusely and then gets up from his chair, heading for an exposed concrete artwork on the opposite wall. His feet are no longer in contact with the floor; he seems to be floating. At first I can't believe it, but the guy really does appear to be flying around the place.

The object is lit from above. He holds his wine glass below the lamp to reassure himself that there aren't any insects floating in his drink. A breath of relief. He battles his way back through a squall of nouveau-riche gallery owners, the squall of nouveau-riche gallery owners in turn battling its way through another squall, this time consisting of the bodyguards surrounding Nicolas Sarkozy's father, who's making his way to the smokers' lounge. I think all over again, every day: the proprietors presumably couldn't make their minds up between a smokers' lounge and a darkroom, although they did make their minds up on a naturalistic vista shot, an Ulrich Seidl shot, so to speak, I don't know. Pamela Anderson enters the freaking place.

I personally would be pleased if you, the audience, found something of use in the evening described above that goes beyond the writer's individual psychology level.

* * *

We place our order. I point with slight embarrassment at the poussin-stuffed mushrooms on the menu.

'How do you get a whole poussin into a tiny mushroom?'

'I'll have two of everything and five bottles of mineral water.'

'Oh, I see now, the poussin's stuffed with mushrooms, not the other way round, sorry.'

'And then I'll have the frozen pistachio stuff for dessert. What is that actually, a new Balkan state?'

'So, Mifti, my experience on the subject you broached: even if you have a behavioural disorder nowadays and even if you're capable of maintaining some semblance of emergency normality, success doesn't come automatically – although your deviant personality makes you a special case.'

Annika's just like, 'Mifti, you've destroyed all language.'

I totally agree but I still ask, 'Why?'

'Everything you promise is a lie, so everything you say is somehow a lie. I really don't care if you ruin your school career and have to go on the game or kill yourself later on. The worst thing is that you're permanently lying to me. You disrespect all the prerequisites of human coexistence. I really don't care if you kill yourself later on or not.'

'Technoplasticity, Annika.'

'What?'

'At some point, once your blood starts circulating on a real technoplastic level, everything's fine again.'

Sure, every girl wants to look like . . .
No actually, I don't want to look like Heidi Klum,
but do her job? Sure. If I was four inches taller?!
(Sexy Julia)

I fight my way through a solid mass of social hardship
on the U8 train, eventually giving up in the face of this
concentrated underclass made of flesh and blood. I come
across Ophelia's former heroin dealer on Oranienstrasse,
head over heels in a container for interim refuse storage.
I remember him as a well-groomed nineteen-year-old of
Russian origin who was utterly clean. Hanging over the
rim of the organic waste bin, he straightens up, looks
more fucked than ever before and raises his hand in
greeting, as if he recognized in me a potential customer
destined for failure in life. Logically enough, that makes
me panic. A moment later he's back on two legs in a
doorway, makes an inconspicuous gesture, and several
junkies not instantly recognizable as such rush towards
him. He smiles over at me. I can't manage to turn my
head away until I've taken a couple of steps in the other
direction. I ring Pörksen's doorbell. His face has been
crowned recently by something he refers to as a strongly
gelled business cut. He's moved in with his permanently
doped-up girlfriend in Kreuzberg. Their new flat is a
failed attempt to lend a serious note to the concept of the

rock 'n' roll lifestyle in the West End of the back of beyond. Rather than emptying the removal boxes, he listens to bad punk at a higher volume than necessary. An extremely large rabbit jumps up to welcome me. It's called Panzer and they brought it back from Denmark when they went surfing there. There was this group of cool guys there, all pretty hardcore, and they had these rabbits with them and they used to let them out now and then, and then these well-dressed guys chased after the rabbits all around the campsite shouting, Panzer, come back, Panzer!

Tina's lying totally incapacitated in front of the TV, watching *Germany's Next Top Model* and shouting now and again with her fingernails buried in her scalp, 'Shit, fuck, wank . . . and all these arsewipes get all the money. That's such a pile of wank, Jesus!'

'What's up?' I ask, not daring to take another look at the greasy-haired entity on the seat behind me. I stare at Pörksen's face to gauge from his reaction to Tina what's going on with her. He shakes his head.

'I can't not eat for four days again, Pörksen!'

'I'm in the top tax bracket this year,' I say.

'Respect!'

I pocket a lump of hash I find lying around and disappear past Tina into the office. Massive sub-woofers – well, at least that's better than some love-sopped gaze – the 'Clitoris Bite Boogie' and a whole load of extremely cheesy Polish disco stuff. Incredible.

I'm like, 'Why does the book put you in a permanent state of sexual arousal?'

'I don't know really, but there's this part in one chapter, for example, where they suddenly start injecting these tiny fish into their veins, so to speak, and that

47

makes them into huge dragons that can fly over the city. I mean, I can really imagine something like that might really exist in thirty years. But it's so awesome that this guy can think up something like that already. Anyway, they shoot up these tiny fishes and turn into these dragons and then they fly around like crazy the whole time, and when they land again they kind of talk about what they could do better next time around. So like one of them says to another one that he shouldn't fly around a certain tower, for example, because they kept getting in each other's way. I can't really tell the story that well, but it's so funny. It kind of symbolizes, like, everything the writer thinks, you know, that Russia's going to reintroduce the monarchy in thirty years' time, so to speak, I don't know.'

'Oh, right!'

'Yeah, well. Tina's read it too.'

Tina is the kind of person who wears a coat made out of the last two surviving Indonesian cave gnus. She does it solely to appear amoral at first glance; a lot of people suddenly feel pure morality is something they vehemently have to combat. I don't want to exercise some moral authority that strikes everyone down with awe. Psychology and morality are not appropriate instruments for dealing with life. There's a popular myth that everything that appears deficient to us can be put down to psychological problems. And morality is unintelligent, it doesn't go far enough. You simply reach a consensus too quickly, people. (That's what occurs to me spontaneously on the subject.)

'Yeah, well, I'm on page seventy-seven or so, but even in chapter two there's this sudden totally cheerful description of a mass rape. I was lying in bed and my vaginal muscles totally cramped up. Completely dumb. I mean, he's writing about the big team they have – the thing about the book is that there's this big team that rules the land, you know what I mean? They're the same ones as with the fish and all that. And then one of them describes this mass rape and he really gets his rocks off.'

'We need a remedial teacher right this instant, if not several!'

I suddenly find myself on a tall bar stool in the middle of an empty living room, an electric guitar pressed into my hands, feeling under pressure, discussing Heidi Klum and the fact that that bitch is imparting medieval standards to my entire generation, and I think: is this the life I wanted to lead when I was thirteen?

Pörksen, a 43-year-old newcomer, screams into the prairies of the music industry he occupies, 'YEAH!'

'D'you fancy a unique mix of village disco and cowboy saloon, Mifti? Imagine Ronald Reagan holding a party in his den!'

Tina's just like, 'And Gorbachev's on the decks!'

And then Pörksen's, like, stuttering like crazy, 'And that's where we're gonna be tonight, little baby. It may be hollow, but it's techno.'

Although I'm absolutely fascinated by decadence coupled with putrefaction and I'm usually pretty stead-fast, I can already envisage myself going under in a huge crowd of libertines who don't want to miss their last chance for uninhibited sex on a Sunday night.

'Hey, shit, why didn't you tell me?'

'Tell you what?'

'Will you look at this crap here.'

'What, it's awesome! Did you watch that video I sent

you, by the way, where the woman says to her husband, "Harald, I'm off to train the dog!" And he's like, "Yeah, yeah, put your coat on, it's chilly out?!"'

'Erm . . .'

'Anyway, there's this weird guy who runs these parties, his name's Ismail and he's a real oddball. Like one time he had this experience, he says there were no drugs involved whatsoever, where his brain just suddenly twisted round. Like, his whole brain matter sort of drifted off to the left, and then there was a hollow space in his head above and below it, and it kind of turned around, so to speak, his brain, and now he sees everything the wrong way round.'

'And do you get used to it?'

'Looks like it, yeah.'

Pörksen knows stuff about a lot of things. Once I was sitting in a car that drove over his heel, and afterwards he was like, 'Don't worry, it's harmless. I saw a documentary about it.'

In my direct vicinity, a bottom with receptive orifices is seeking a hot stallion for regular orifice training. The people here like giving head and they also fuck untiringly to reggae before my very eyes, all part and parcel of a displacement activity lasting several years in total. In this black-painted basement grotto, the logical assumption is that you've landed up in some nether anti-world. So that's the point I'm at right now; some of the guests are wearing Venetian masks and the theme is unexplored territories, and this kind of thing so doesn't fascinate me. There's not enough space for uncoordinated monging on the simulated dance floor, seeing as there are far too many contorted people present who've come to tonight's party without any particular fetish. I drink vodka and cranberry juice on a steel seat, not moving a muscle and breathing in as rarely as possible so as not to inhale anything unexpected. A girl is hanging from the ceiling on a chain, her shoulders dislocated, stretchmarks across her back. Of course, we don't feel justified not to categorize her screams as part of the whole show.

It's a parallel world. We're sitting next to a woman who calls herself Smiley Susie and her guy. The two of them are around fifty with tattoos across their shaved heads. 'Mifti, listen for a minute. I've known Smiley Susie since primary school days! She used to sit on a bench at gymnastics all on her own in a pale blue towelling leotard.'

There's this hole in the guy's lower arm.

'I was hungry.' 'What?' 'I was hungry so I cut a chunk out of my arm. Anyway, d'you know Tuffi?' 'What?' 'The elephant that jumped out of the monorail over Wuppertal in the sixties?'

'WHAT?'

'You don't know him then, never mind. There was this circus elephant, right, and they walked him through the monorail as an advertising gag and then he only went and jumped out. It's suspended, you know.' 'ZEN, darling, Zen.' 'What's Zen?' 'Let me spell it for you: Z-E-N. You know, as in Zen Buddhism, and Zen's this state of mind, totally meditative, and you don't care about anything. But while you're at it you do sometimes think about stuff you're supposed to do and—' 'What?' 'You think of stuff you're supposed to do, right, like buy toilet paper, and this guy who organizes meditation trips with fifty people, right, he told me one time that you just have to say to yourself, goodbye, I have to buy toilet paper.' 'WHAT?' 'Goodbye, I have to buy toilet paper.'

It's only now that I realize nobody here has a face. It's a really clever lighting solution, albeit an unfathomable one: nobody has a face, there's an atmosphere of unlimited anonymity. So it's all about God here.

You're only anonymous at this party, and you're only anonymous if you're God.

An inferno. Hell on earth. Sex is always an act of violence anyway. Eusebius of Caesarea says: 'Woe betide him who considers hell risible now and must experience Hell himself before he believes in it.'

And even though, being an enlightened human being, I've long interpreted hell as an instrument of political power, I now believe in it. From one second to the next, I'm somewhere else. In a television documentary on Siberia, where scientists doing a test drilling to research the origin of earthquakes reach a cavity nine kilometres under the earth. They let down a microphone into the chamber. The sound of human screams comes over the microphone. Countless voices. And later a cloud of poisonous gas escapes from the hole they drilled. Even the tiniest sound penetrates to my inner ear through the labyrinth of bone and I make out the voices, and they're telling me something that definitely wasn't premeditated by whoever created this track. The music and me and a terrifying creature with a hideous face and claws, which appears as they retrieve the drill head and hisses at me, making me leave my place in panic.

I've never looked at Pörksen the way I am now, his tongue just about in my pharynx, his eyes screwed shut an inch away from mine. Actually none of it would interest me in the slightest if it weren't for this pure horniness taking me over right now. We're sitting on a seat full of holes with yellow foam emerging from them. I get a face full of artificial fog, tears run down my cheeks, and by the time I can see again and want to pull his face back to mine he's disappeared.

'Oi, you, I think someone's waiting for you outside,' says Smiley Susie.

'Ho ho ho! Amazing day: sun, sea, beach, wind, happy dog, happy Susie.'

'How old is she?'

'Did you know they have VIP nights here?'

'You pay twenty thousand euros and you get to shag a sheikh up the arse.'

Everyone's a foot taller than me and I get a constant series of armpits in my face as I rush outside. And then he's standing there smoking, and I wonder if this is all about drugs or sex or a nice cool night breeze. He comes towards me, I take the cigarette out of his hand, and as I take a drag he bites my neck. At some point I'm lying on the wet concrete ground with my legs akimbo, gravel aggregate digging into my back. Pörksen on top of me, my sequinned tights round my ankles. In this position, I let him fuck me in the mouth for an incredible length of time, for various reasons. As the sun rises, warm cum runs down my throat. It disgorges all over my face; funnily enough there's something pretty operatic about it. I turn my head slightly to the left, very slowly. For some reason I can't fathom, the movement causes an extremely loud, threatening sound as if I were in an open quarry, just about to be crushed by a landslide. This is it. The ground kind of turns soft, hot, I don't know if it's my back that rips open or the ground beneath me, and when Pörksen says, 'Look, Mifti, d'you think that was a bat that made an echo off the TV tower by flapping its wings?' the volume of his voice rises exponentially like you wouldn't believe and it turns into a giant snarling that I've been expecting all along anyway. It's just far too loud. Pins and needles pierce my eardrums. Thick, dark red tube-like structures protrude from my arms. Veins with tiny insects squishing through them. They get bigger and bigger until my blood vessels burst and dark maggots come creeping out of my body, crawling over me, mutating into flat beetles with feelers three times as long as their abdomens.

The taxi driver says, 'I've driven you before, haven't I?'
  'Pardon?'
  'It's your teeth and your eyes, I've seen them before.'
  'Yeah, a crossbite, pretty tragic.'

I limp into the flat, blood seeping from my lip in all seriousness, which gets me totally worried again. A hyped-up Edmond is wolfing down liquorice wheels in the kitchen. Annika's asleep, lying innocently and heart-wrenchingly ready for sacrifice under one of our covers printed with comic characters. Her life of regularity moves me to a spontaneous attack of sentimentality. I decide I will never again get into a situation that transforms her face into a concerned battlefield of contradictions.
  'Have we got any halloumi left?' I ask Edmond, and he turns to face me with his eyes wide.
  'Yeah, probably.'

'Can you fry it up for me?'

'Can't you fry it yourself?'

'No.'

'OK.'

'So you'll do it?'

'Only if you watch to see how to do it.'

I tiptoe into my room, still in an absolute panic that the floor will open up and swallow me any minute now.

'COME BACK HERE AND WATCH THIS, WILL YOU, MIFTI!'

'NO!'

'Huh?'

'I'm so dizzy.'

'Oh.'

There is hope for us all
(Nick Lowe)

Pörksen's parents are apparently complete esoteric hippies, which is why he's pretty agnostic about my current astral travel phase. This is now my twelfth attempt to leave my body, except I keep getting slung back into the darkness of my completely blacked-out bedroom by this crazy shortness of breath. It's 12:45 and I've done nothing for the past five hours but lie in bed smoking. The only light source consists of the glow of my cigarette every time I take a drag. I look down my body and suddenly think I'm only occupying this thing here temporarily, the thing with the lungs and all the blood vessels and that, like a parasite from another star system come for research reasons to ... well, anyway. At any rate, a few hours ago I was suddenly not inside it any more for a tiny moment. I severed myself from it as this weird cloud-like shell or as air, and I felt the exact moment when I was dragged back into the mouldering old thing by a power beyond my possession. I can't take this any more. That power is God. I hate God.

Pörksen calls. He says, 'Jesus, at some point you just started mumbling, fuck ... err ... fuck, baby, what's going on? Wow. Anyway first you did this completely hardcore thingying around, then you sucked me off when we got home, and at some point you ripped Tina's Pavel Pepperstein picture off the wall. It's OK, though, thank God. And after that we heard this weird noise, and you—'

'What d'you mean, when we got home?'

'Back to my place, you know.'

'We were outside.'

'You're just a bit confused, hon.'

'What?'

'You spent precisely two seconds outside yesterday. On the walk to and from the taxi.'

'I think something's going into meltdown here, Pörksen.'

'Anyway, at about five a.m. we heard this crazy noise like someone snoring their head off, and then suddenly something flew away, it was a—'

'Pörksen, if we really did go back to your place, that means something's up with my perception of time and space. And don't you try and neutralize it with the word psychosis. All last night's gone into meltdown, I swear. I could swear we were outside. You were kneeling over me, and the ground opened up, that's what happened.'

'And what's that supposed to mean? That you've understood the world as a whole? Believe me, I've been there already. The only mistake mankind ever made was inventing time – I found that totally plausible back then.'

'I—'

'You were totally strange yesterday, Mifti. And you hadn't even taken anything, that's the weird thing. What a comedown. You're lucky we took you back with us. Someone could have totally cut your guts out of your body, and then you'd have woken up later with an arsehole the size of Canada. Or not. You never know what might happen in a situation like that, it's in God's hands.'

'Where's Annika?'

'At work.' Edmond is kind of bouncing aimlessly around the flat.

'OK, so did she say anything? Like when's she coming home? Hel-looo?'

'All she said was that you were lying in bed with totally dilated pupils and that she doesn't know quite how you're supposed to get out of your tricky situation. You're really infuriating her, Mifti. What are you trying to prove? That you can ruthlessly cut all the ties to your relatives without even showing the slightest sign of emotion? And she told me to tell you that you don't have to sell your own grandmother. You don't have to sell your grandmother and you do have to go to school. You have to just get down to it. That's an imploring request. I want to know who you really are.'

'What are you talking about? And why can't she tell me all that to my face? I'm sitting here and you're telling me that she told you that I don't have to sell my own grandmother.'

'And you didn't empty the dishwasher either. She asked if it's pure evil or fear that makes you do it.'

'Like I so give a fuck if I emptied the dishwasher or not! Of course you have to take her side, you can't help it. Unfortunately you live out of her pocket, you have no other option but to underscore her conspiracy theories against me with loud-mouthed endorsements, but just look at me will you! I'm a girl of small means and I'm completely fucked up, and she comes along and expects me to function perfectly, but I can't. I don't just function properly like a happy little bunny, I don't function at all. Material greed, rituals and habits, jealousy, a lack of privacy, it's all coveting, coveting, coveting.'

'Maybe it's time you went to see a therapist.'

'I know if they want you to draw trees you mustn't make the roots too thick, because that's a sign of aggression. Too many fruits mean you're over-striving, too many flowers mean you're overly romantic. You can totally rule out finding anything out about me that way – forget it.'

Is that what you all class as insanity? Are you scared of going insane? Do people who go crazy send nice warm shivers down your spine?

By the way, the fact that Edmond appears so concentrated with regard to my recent misbehaviour shocks me to death. I'm plagued by self-doubt. He's not the disinterested arsehole I've known all my life any more.

We set the table on the balcony with a flourish – plastic-wrapped ham and cheese slices past their sell-by date – talking about how his fringe theatre crap might develop into something that . . . well, something anyway, maybe something that enables him to get a second home in Costa Rica.

'So, Mifti, right, in the beginning you have all these endless possibilities, and suddenly your options get more and more restricted, so it meant I had to set boundaries for myself, and suddenly you realize, oh shit, no, you have to block it and it's completely dumb, the guy could have staged an excellent performance without all that post-structuralist crap about the concept of happiness and the one-size-fits-all moral crap. I was like totally blown away by the whole thing, so I'm just standing there and thinking, wow, it's so totally touching and great, and then I started talking about that abstruse mass rape in scene four and I was still totally euphoric and then I looked at the actors and they're just like, yeah, umm. D'you get what I mean?'

'You want to do theatre, yeah, of course, and there are all these rules for the theatre, even if they're completely dumb rules like the one where one actor's not supposed to stand in front of another one. That's what the director used to be there for, so he could tell them: you can't see the others from the front if you stand like that. I mean I'm not the kind of person who thinks everything's just a game, but if you look at a play as this funny kind of game, then logic dictates you have to look at it conventionally as a stupid childhood game, even though you can't project yourself back into your whole idyllic childhood – and you want something else, you don't just want to play "Ring-a-Ring o' Roses". So you can't ever really go back there, but you can take the attitude that anything goes. So you don't waste time thinking about whether you ought to subjugate yourself to certain standards or techniques. Anything goes on stage, you're allowed to disregard all the classic forms within the problem of content, all the moral laws and any kind of technique. The whole social network that's involved is the equivalent of a fifteen-month-old baby in its early childhood omnipotence phase.'

'I don't quite get what you mean.'

'There's just this one world of natural laws, one world of social laws and constraints, one world of moral laws and conventions and there's this one world of games and pretences. And because theatre's a social art, you never know whether it's really all that free, because in some sense it's also a societal confrontation between people in their roles in society. So it has to remain communicable. Although – actually, it doesn't. If you have the possibility to make a completely off-the-wall work of art you don't even need an audience.'

'So what happens if you exchange the world of social laws for the world of games and pretences in your private life? That's what we do all the time, isn't it?'

'No idea. But I definitely think we're far more than an insider phenomenon now.'

'That's just what I keep asking myself. You do theatre because you want to have fun, kind of thing, but when I put on that piece in Brussels and it was so expensive, I don't know, and anyway there was this guy there and he goes, "So, did you have fun?" And I was like totally glad he asked me that, because I looked so unhappy. And that's something where I think, do I stay true to the whole thing or do I stay true to myself, and if I stay true to myself will I ever find a room in a flatshare? And then you meet people who think just as many thoughts about the whole thing or about some other subject, but that doesn't matter really, as long as somebody somewhere is thinking thoughts at all, whether it's about raccoon livers or Medea.'

'As long as you're having fun, kind of thing.'

'Yeah, and you know, I just, when we were in Brussels, and that was the only moment while I was staying in Belgium that I thought, yeah, the thing with the mass rape scene went really well.'

'I have no lack of ideas, and you have no lack of radicalism and no lack of courage. The one and only thing you lack is influential people who you can convince of what you do, Edmond.'

He smiles triumphantly, I eat half-fat margarine by the ton with candied spiders, and then we clear the table the way happy little bunnies do these things. At some point Edmond asks me if I fancy biscuits shaped like animals, and I reach into the bag he presents and pull out an elephant.

'Oh no, you can't eat that one.'

'Sorry?'

'It's a protected species. The Malayan *elephas maximus*.'

Dear Medea,

Whatever happened to you? A character in a drama who has a problem with her lover, essentially nothing more than a stomping ethnic minority womb who kills her children during a spontaneous emotional outburst at the Deutsches Theater, and in a fitted kitchen, and in the nineteenth century. I'm firmly convinced that you didn't sink back into your uterus plagued to death by female jealousy – you were a politician. Murdering your children was a coldly calculated political act.

You demanded your human rights by means of a claim for justice that developed by necessity into the murder of your children, in this society. You had a right to fame and dignity, and you weren't just mere female biology, dependent on a lover. You were related to a sun god.

All my love,
Mifti

Alice, I'm just thinking about you right now and I'm not going to stop either seeing your face or writing these things down, because otherwise it'll all be gone, this directness will be gone and this happiness too. But I'm still never going to have anything to do with you again, because you obviously don't want to love me any more, regardless of whether the circumstances are to blame or not. There are complications, because I tend to act like a little child. All this is probably way off the mark, of course there are shades of grey, but you're still there somewhere – why don't you come out, you hackneyed old whore?

Annika's pubes are in a shocking state. She apologizes for them as she gets in the bathtub with me, and we're sisters again. We're sisters who'd have nothing to hide from one other if only we were both passionate student teachers specializing in sport.

As she now informs me, today I puked up next to Edmond's anodized aluminium keyboard and knocked the living room table over. Just for a change, she's not standing in the background troubled by moral concerns, but rubbing in eucalyptus shower lotion and essential oils, lying in a calming bath completely off her head.

'You know I'm going away tomorrow, don't you Mifti?'

'No, you weird fascinating monster dictator.'

Annika explains that our world is in constant flux and trends are the trailblazers of this process of change. So as to ride the crest of the wave and not have to react to tides, she and her agency maintain an international network – the majority of whom will spend tomorrow making a deliberately ironic music video for the agency's Facebook page at a fancy-dress party with the theme 'Strange in Brandenburg'. As part of the event, thirty to forty poorly paid 'PR trainees with their fingers on the fashion pulse' will be singing Alice Cooper's 'Poison', 'showcasing the high-quality summer collections of the labels they represent on a continuous basis'. The whole thing was initiated by Annika herself. She's simply the one who knows best how to come up with experiential worlds and couple her market-friendly intellect with her experience of innovative marketing tools.

'You know, don't you, we're on a constant hunt for trends and changes.'

'Oh, right. And when are you coming back? D'you think my teeth look kind of funny?'

'Huh? No?!'

'Phew.'

'Next week.'

'Why next week? What are you doing out there for so long? You'll come back home and sleep for three weeks solid. You can't do that to us, Annika.'

'I don't even want to do that to you. We have to have conferences and that. I just think it's pretty wicked shit.'

'Yeah, it's wicked shit.'

Suddenly Edmond tears the bathroom door open and yells with joyful aplomb, 'FUCKING DRUGHEADS!'

Annika yells back, 'FUCKING DRUGHEAD!' and throws the dumb shower lotion stuff at him, which misses Edmond but hits the doorframe and will leave traces of its contents on our hall carpet for the next four years.

I say, 'Edmond, can you please leave the bathroom, I'd like to concentrate on our unacceptable state as such right now.'

He leaps into the bathtub fully clothed. I flip out completely. Annika laughs over-ambitious and uninhibitedly despairing tears. Edmond is wearing turquoise Doc Martens, in which he very recently stomped through a nearby piece of woodland. Mud and particles of dog shit float in the bathwater. He tries to adopt a position that might prove acceptable for all parties. Now he's sitting calmly between us, first of all taking a deep breath of course.

'Mifti?'

'Yeah?'

'Can you give me my money back now? Are you feeling better now?'

'Huh?'

At this point we're informed that I not only puked up next to Edmond's anodized aluminium keyboard but also refused (just as unscrupulously) to repay my debts to him from the previous day, with the argument, 'Fuck capitalism!'

'But what debts anyway?'

'Well, not exactly debts, but I gave you the money to buy that thing, you know.'

'What thing exactly?'

'An international culture magazine.'

'And now?'

'Now I want my change, kind of thing.'

'Oh right, sorry, I'll just go and get it.'

I run to my purse, only to find that I kind of haven't got enough for some reason. I run back, by which point Edmond has calmly shoved an oversized chocolate-coated soft marshmallow traditionally known in Germany as a 'nigger's kiss' into Annika's face and is now bent over her ribs inspecting her tonsils for white spots.

'That looks pretty cool from here – if Annika wasn't naked I'd take a photo.'

'I've got this sore throat out of nowhere, Mifti. I don't know how come. Edmond's just checking if I've got white spots on my tonsils.'

'So how much do I get back now? You know – interest. One dumpling for every week.'

I press a small amount of change into his hand.

'Are you kidding me, Mifti?'

Annika: 'Edmond, what d'you think, men in underpants and socks are the worst, aren't they?'

Edmond: 'I just can't stand my own sexiness, I always have to take the sting out of it so I don't get a boner every time I look in the mirror.'

Mifti: 'Well, I bought that book about the Baader-Meinhof gang, the one you told me to get, where the woman describes it all from her perspective, and then your international wank thing, and they both cost seventeen euro. So I spent thirty-four euro altogether, and now you get nine euro back.'

'But I gave you a fifty-euro note!'

'I won't listen if you shout like that!'

'Fifty euro, Mifti!'

'Yeah, but then I bought cigarettes as well, because you smoked all mine the other day.'

'But we're still not back to the original fifty euro.'

'There's a minimal deficit.'

'And where is that?'

'In my jacket pocket.'

And there it is: the sound, your access to absolutely any state of consciousness you desire. Anything you want can be produced at short notice, the blackness before your eyes occasionally rent by brief flickers. It's all about your gimpish grin and those moments of unstoppable loss of yourself, confirming nothing other than that you're no longer an individual human being in this mass of polytoxicomaniacs wading spasmodically through the shit, but a dissolving piece of commonality. You're dissolving, you let yourself bounce off one wall to the next and then into the arms of the bass that allows you everything you want. It infiltrates your muscles and you beam at it, driven to the extremest of extremes by the violation of the basic rules you once set yourself.

Edmond: 'It's so fucking secondary that you're so fucking symbiotic.'
   'WE'RE NOT FUCKING SYMBIOTIC!'

I open my eyes, take a sidestep to the left because of my loss of balance and slam backwards against our front door. I take three steps forwards and slam backwards against some kind of ice cream advertising medium set up in the public sphere. I turn around and slam backwards against an acne-ridden guy in a green uniform. The police officer's progress in terms of non-verbal communication goes like this: he drags me roughly down a stone staircase – how on earth did I get here? – he shoves me in a taxi, the taxi driver drives off and is inspired to turn the radio up out of identification with his aggressor (which is me). I feel transported back to a four-thousand-capacity establishment and start to cry as George Michael wails hysterically 'Guilty feet ain't got no rhythm' at me from the speakers – in a track that makes me suddenly want to give anything for a 2×2 metre laminate dance floor. I wail along, still crying, the driver asking me for the third time, 'Where am I supposed to take you then?'

I take three steps back and slam backwards against the taxi. I lie down in the entrance to the former factory building where Ophelia lives, finally falling victim to an unspecific emotional articulation generally categorized as facial expression and accompanied by floods of tears. Crying is not attached to any particular emotion, occurring frequently, however, in cases of fear, melancholy and aggression, for example. Those who rampage tend to wreak blind destruction. Those who are traumatized (in the broadest sense) tend to find themselves constantly in situations of heightened nervousness.

I'm standing misplaced in the washroom, eyeing a systematically heterogeneous group of filamentous fungal growths stretching in snaking lines across an organic substance as a greenish coating. My kindergarten's going mouldy. I'm four years old and very recently puked into the open palms of a trainee nursery nurse.

I'm standing crying in my mother's bedroom as two china dishes containing my milk teeth and unfounded accusations are slung in my face. She says she's going to die. She severs the back of my knee with a spare cutter blade. She severs my tendons with a lightness of hand, she cuts up everything that belongs to me in the slightest, she sets fire to my open wounds with an extra-long refillable electronic lighter printed with an advertisement for cling film and fitted with a child lock. She says I'm the best thing that ever happened to her. SHE SAYS I'M THE BEST THING THAT EVER HAPPENED TO HER.

* * *

I say to Alice, 'Maybe I've got borderline personality disorder.'

Alice answers, 'Oh, that whole borderline personality syndrome crap is the equivalent of unspecified upper stomach pain. They always say that when they can't think of anything else.'

I'm sitting in the church hall of the Düsseldorf-Düsseltal Lutheran Community at the age of six, compelled to celebrate Christmas at an event organized by my teacher. Yellow laminate floor, brown curtains, woodchip wallpaper and homemade posters. My mother gives me two Santas made of Kinder Surprise eggs and cotton wool. I pretend to be moved to tears.

'Can you see all the crap lying around here? That paper and foil over there?' she asks.

I nod.

'The other parents all gave their children these Santas, and they just went and broke them because they were so greedy for the bloody chocolate. Their parents went to so much trouble, and the little bastards just go and smash the Santas and chuck them in the corner.'

My mother starts crying. I hug her. There are no perpetrators, only victims. The younger a child is, the more guilty. The more responsible a child is for his or her sociopath parent, the better he or she can deal with his or her own criminal liability.

0:08. Perhaps you're only innocent when you have no idea of morals any more, I think at some point, finding myself completely unlikeable. I really need to get out of this habit of precociousness before it takes on a life of its own. By the time Ophelia says hello through the intercom I appear as if the pain were either non-existent or already processed. Four storeys and a woman who only values our spiritual kinship for her own sake. She's standing in the doorway smoking, wearing a pink and blue striped satin nightshirt.

'You smoke too much, Mifti!'

'Why? Because I'm so out of breath?'

'Yeah. And you know what? I think it's so great, the whole idea of the two of us as a culture annihilation crew.'

Ophelia's converted warehouse and industrial space is 290 square metres in total. The floor is concrete, the walls are four-centimetre-thick plasterboard. Her art collection is dominated by genre and landscape painting, with almost no trace of religious motifs or the intensified post-1970s modernism-postmodernism discussion. She bundles me on to one of her seats, offers me a probiotic yoghurt and asks, 'Why exactly are you here right now?'

I shrug. Were I capable of crying in the presence of people made of flesh and blood and not only in my own company, a number of things would be easier, both for myself and for the people made of flesh and blood.

'Mifti, you're too good, too young, too promising, too talented. I'll scare you right out of here if you put on some great big performance. I scare off everyone I love, and then I feel something too. I went to Salem boarding school. Salem's totally pathetic, at the end of the day. I did everything right but nothing works. That's where I perfected my asocial streak, camouflaged under the façade of my empathy. I'm the same age as everyone when they die. That's why you're the superior one.'

I don't say anything.

'Is all this crap here something to do with your mother

again? Don't you want to tell me what your mother was like?'

'On benefits, permanently wasted, Chanel suits despite it all.'

'And what's happened now?'

'I went to that unexplored territories party with Pörksen and Tina yesterday.'

'Why didn't you text me? A good day to rattle, wrestle and fight or punch guts.'

'What?'

'Yeah, Mifti, someone asked me there one time if he could ram this big fuck-off medieval fork into my sternum. And of course I put up inconspicuous resistance and pretended I had an urgent appointment at the bar – you always do that, don't you, pretend you really really need to go to the bar – but the whole situation proved all over again that anything goes. Not only can you shove aubergines up arseholes, you can try to ram four metal spikes into the flesh under a complete stranger's jaws.'

'Anyway I went there.'

'Yeah, that's where we were just now.'

'And it was completely OK, even though I was utterly fazed by all the shaven-headed fetish freaks. What I'm getting at, this afternoon I completely flipped out, even though I got up this morning and felt amazingly fine under the circumstances. I was putting up these shelves with Edmond, and everything was totally chilled and great and wicked, and I thought, hey, yeah, family and that. And then some bit of wood broke off, and it totally freaked me out. Some stupid bastard little piece of wood broke off the freaking shelves, and I just stood there and started screaming at Edmond, and I thought it was the end of the world. And then I even called my father and said, "Dad, oh shit, it's all too late."

'And he's like, "Can you please start the conversation properly?"

'"Dad, can I talk to you a minute?"

'And he's just like, "How much money do you want?"

'"I'm in real shit here, something's just broken off." And no one knew what was going on. Not even I knew. And I can't remember the rest. And then at some point Annika threw me out. She didn't use violence, she didn't present a horrific challenge for the law enforcement authorities by beating me out of the front door, she just threw me out. That's how fucked I was. And now I'm here.'

'How did you get here?'

'Some railway policeman put me in a taxi. I stumbled into his arms completely fucked-up.'

'And how did you pay for the taxi? Is there some hysterical professional chauffeur leaping around my backyard who I have to pay off?'

'No. I had some money in my shoe, no idea why, but I still had money in my shoe.'

Ophelia gives a nod of respect and gets up. She drinks a large glass of tap water before she ventures any reaction: 'Why are you here?'

'Because yours was the only address I could think of.'

Ophelia gives another nod of respect and sits down again.

'I kind of can't find any way to react. I hope you don't expect any reaction. I can tell you, go to school, don't take heroin, integrate into your family structure as well as possible and be a surgeon when you grow up. Just get down to it.'

'D'you know how often I hear that, Ophelia? That I should just get down to it?'

'I don't even want to tell you all that stuff. I've always thought I'm the one who's the child. You don't have to defend your mother even though she's dead and she was a great woman, you don't have to feel responsible for your father or his well-being or the fact that he can exist without having to think about whether you exist, and if he does then of course he thinks you only exist in a state of total lack of needs. I know that feeling. Sitting staring at some box of pills just because some bastard couldn't keep his prick to himself, because Mummy . . . well, what? Shouldn't have had children? Should have stayed her mother's little baby rather than becoming the mother of her own little baby? Should they not have left you and me with our mothers? They were with us, Holy Saint Mifti, we weren't with them. It tastes like shit, like metal, it tastes bitter, and it definitely doesn't taste of comfort, but maybe it tastes of meaning in a general mouldering way.'

Ophelia makes a kitsch waving-it-off gesture, signalling that she's emotionally unstable and too drunk to maintain the conversation. She takes a pea-sized plastic sphere out of the breast pocket of her nightshirt and chucks it over at me. I chuck it back again.

'By the way, I met your old crazy dealer the other day,' I say.

Instead of answering me, she peels off the plastic film. In the end there's a pinch of brownish powder on the mahogany table, looking like instant tea and smelling like a mixture of cigarette butts, trash and vinegar. She rolls a tube out of a piece of silver foil, tipping half the powder on to another piece. When she holds a lighter

73

under the foil, the heroin melts, producing a miniature trail of smoke. Ophelia inhales this vapour with the aid of the aforementioned aluminium tube, until all that remains is something very dirty, small and evil, and she asks me, 'So what do my pupils look like now?'

'Jesus, shit, I'm underage.'

'No, Mifti. You're not sixteen, you're an indirect extension of my life now.'

Her head drifts slowly towards the tabletop. I stroke her back and wait until she regains control over her body, put out of service by a sudden alteration in perception. It takes an eternity.

'Or more like a direct extension. Mifti?'

'Yes?'

'I'll get you an invitation and you can come to Samantha and Albrecht's party in Charlottenburg next Friday. It's their wedding reception, completely fucked up, what d'you expect in Charlottenburg? Emre's DJing. He eats black pudding sandwiches. I hate eating meat, but sometimes, every so often, I get these wild cravings for dirty great black pudding sandwiches.'

'Can you get hold of some coke?'

'I don't spend money any more on drugs that don't make music sound good.'

'But I really need to do coke again, Ophelia. When you're bored, and I am right now, or at least I would be if we weren't sitting here together, but anyway – when you're bored you always think of drugs right away, don't you?'

'I love you, Mifti.'

'Who's Emre anyway?'

'The man of my life.'

'And what's he like?'

'On benefits, permanently wasted, Chanel suit.'

* * *

At 3:55 a.m. I wake up on Ophelia's bedroom floor and decide to leave her apartment without passing Go. Ophelia's heavy-breathing on top of her double bed, which is covered in puke. I scrabble around the room, collecting up enough coins for cigarettes and a short-hop train ticket out of strategically placed porcelain dishes filled with five-cent pieces. Once I've closed the bedroom door as quietly as possible, I sprint along the mile-long corridor towards the exit, both hands full of small change. From one second to the next I start suffering from a psychological disorder accompanied by a temporary loss of connection to reality: I hear voices. I get hysterical. Hallucinations are clear symptoms of psychosis. I regard not myself but my surroundings as altered and can't recognize my abnormal condition; that's what occurs to me spontaneously right now. The voices are coming from the kitchen, only a few hours ago still smoked up with heroin trails, and they're talking about an art form that finds its expression in the production of moving images: 'Well, perhaps you can walk over there, OK. Then I'd like you to act out recognizing your own desperation in Marie's anger.'

When I enter the kitchen, there are fifteen people standing around, either talking about the contradictions in their roles or correcting backlit lighting effects.

I ask, 'Excuse me, but what's going down here?'

They look at me as if I were the world's thinnest-skinned person.

'I know there's nobody who's NOT staring at me as if I was the world's thinnest-skinned person, but what's happening here right now? Have you talked to Ophelia about it?'

A stick-thin unit manager in a cheap brand of jeans looks over at me with such an ominous expression that I fall suddenly silent and creep inconspicuously out of the kitchen and back to Ophelia's bedroom. I wrench the door open and scream, 'Ophelia, there are fifteen people in your kitchen!'

She wakes up with a jerk and throws the same freaking shoe at me that she threw over the door of a toilet cubicle last week. Then she sinks back on to her feather pillows.

'What's going down, Ophelia? There's fifteen people in your kitchen.'

'Are they really here already?'

'Yes, they're really here already!'

'Have they got cameras and lights and stuff with them?'

'I think so.'

'Then my friend Frauke's filming a scene for her final exam project, where this guy puts cyanide in his girlfriend's tampon so that she dies. Wicked, huh? As long as people make a film in my apartment it's guaranteed to stand out from all that young German social realism crap.'

Back in the kitchen, I help myself bold as brass from the buffet spread across a trestle table. Nobody takes any notice as I eat a roll spread with nutella and watch a heavily made-up woman in fishnet tights screaming, 'Just give up your fucking drugs, Jürgen! I don't want any fucking drugs in my place!'

Jürgen is played by a man completely undisturbed by the hand-held camera close to his face, sniffing blueish powder.

I say, 'That doesn't look very realistic, does it, if you

76

want to make a drugs film and he's snorting blueish powder. What's that supposed to be then?'

'Fuck, who are you anyway?'

'D'you mind if I use the bathroom for a minute?'

'No, you can't go in there, someone's getting high-collagen tissue painted on their back in there right now.'

I stomp angrily across the middle of the kitchen, say, 'Go bury your fucking film in the desert then!' and slam the front door behind me.

Mental blackout.

I shout, 'Hey, fuck, who shat in your brain?'

Annika flinches. At 7:20 a.m. she conscientiously emptied a bucket of water over me as I lay weeping in my bed.

'Oh God, sorry, Mifti, I didn't notice you were awake. Why are you crying?'

'Yeah, fuck, would you look at my hair now!'

'Come on, Mifti, we have to get this over with, come on now! You look so great, don't cry, please!'

Of course Annika can totally understand that I'm crying now and I don't understand the world any more and don't recognize myself.

'You look really great.'

'No, I've got all these complexes and my hair just gave me this special strength.'

'Honey, look at yourself. You're really confident . . .'

'I'm not confident at all.'

'We both have no confidence and together we're strong, me with my nasty fat tummy and now you with your funny hair which looks completely gorgeous.'

'That's what I'd say now if I was you.'

'You look good, I'm not kidding, you look like Carmen Electra in a lagoon!'

'Really?'

Annika sits down on the side of the bed, smiling and taking my hand.

'But you really have to get up now, it's twenty past seven.'

'Hey, come on, just let me sleep another five minutes.'

'What's up with you? Are you sick? D'you want to stay in bed all day again or what?'

'I told you I'm getting up.'

'You promised me you'd go to school today. This is really the end of the line.'

'No, it's not the end at all, just let me stay in bed another thirty seconds, look, I'm counting to thirty.'

I really do count out loud up to twenty-two.

'Your thirty seconds are up.'

'THREE MINUTES, ANNIKA!'

'NO! NO!'

'You're yelling at me the whole time and bombarding me with freaking orders and you seriously expect me to get up?'

'What d'you expect me to do then, baby sister? Should I beat you out of bed or what? D'you want me to beat you up? I can't beat you up, though, sorry, that's out of the question I'm afraid.'

'Of course you can.'

She gives me a shocked look. 'No.'

'Of course you can, Annika, just go ahead and beat me up.'

Within a matter of seconds, her shock transfigures into limitless understanding for every single violent parent and guardian on the planet. She's struggling, she hates me, she's capable of forcing me back with traditional unconcern into a position in which I spent years of my life longing for repression and humiliation. As soon as she touches me I'm all hers. We watch each other dying in silence for three long minutes.

'No, I can't,' she says and turns away. I pull the cover over my head and start to cry again.

'You're trying to turn me into your sick, dead, sadistic fucking mother. I'm totally paranoid. You killed your mother and you'll end up killing me, that's what my freaking paranoia keeps telling me.'

'I didn't kill my mother.'

'You were born; you killed her. It's as simple as that.'

'She said I was the best thing that ever happened to her.'

'She ripped open your oesophagus with the screw of a choke pear. Would you just stop letting these pseudo-naive, pseudo-childish, pseudo-innocent statements out of the wall of your teeth. You're gonna make me puke, I swear. You're not the abused three-year-old you constantly pretend to be in your constant pseudo-trauma. There aren't any vivid memories left inside you that have developed an ominous life of their own and are now turning on you. You're the one who's turning on us. You're grown up, Mifti.'

'Jesus, get you. Quite the amateur psychologist.'

'You're just demanding your right to be tortured, am I right?'

'Yeah, great.'

You're dragged out of bed and across the parquet flooring by your three-year-old pseudo-traumatized hair and after a few minutes of total lack of orientation you find yourself under your half-sister's shin, she having discovered her sadistic side and attempting to smash the back of your head in with her elbow. She's kneeling on my back because, unlike me myself, my body is a bundle

79

of reflexes reacting to physical pain that can't hold still. I scream. Even the screaming has nothing to do with me, it's to do with my system's direct reaction to a particular stimulus. I am not my screams, I am not my physical reaction to pain, I am not an animal. Funnily enough, I'm hungry. You always think of the most banal things in this kind of situation. Something really odd happened to me two weeks ago. I was walking down Choriner Strasse one night and this mega-aggressive gang of chavs turns up on the other side of the road. Wearing baseball caps, their socks tucked into their cheap jeans and with this severely underage minger in 10-euro pointy stilettos in tow. Prompted by a joint surplus of ideas they decide to throw an empty beer bottle in my direction. I put my headphones on. The second bottle landed right in front of my feet, and the guys crossed over the road.

'Stop where you are, you haven't got a chance,' said the most hideous one of them, as I was still clinging to the belief that I could beat the lot of them to a pulp with a couple of skilful kicks. And then someone kicked his foot into my sight line from behind, and I just managed to dodge it. The only thing I thought of was all the numbers on my mobile phone. Not my mobile. Please not my mobile.

And then the hideous one's like, 'Oi, you just did a Nazi salute or what?'

'Pardon?'

'I saw you, you just did a Nazi salute!'

'No I didn't.'

'I saw you, don't gimme that!'

'Are you crazy? I put my headphones on – I'm not even German!'

The chavs' faces froze, and then they relaxed again and all looked pretty confused.

'Shit, sorry, we thought you's a Nazi.'

'No way! Hey, you can't just go rocking down Choriner Strasse and beating people up.'

'Nah, we always do that. Erhan gives them a high kick, and then when they're down on the ground, all the rest of us pile in.'

Erhan's like, 'Yeah, sorry about that kick, but at least I missed.'

'Can we get a couple of cigarettes off you?'

My head's bleeding. I'm calmer than ever before. I'm lying on my stomach, clearly identifiable as a victim, savouring the state of total freedom from responsibility. Utter innocence because the whole fucking thing is a particularly severe violation of the child's well-being. I'm evidently a child and thus entitled to well-being, and evidently my well-being as a child is being proved to me by being violated. I'm evidently sufficiently independent of Annika to recognize only the advantages arising for me as a result of her criminally prosecutable actions. I'm sufficiently independent of my sister to hyperventilate in her face that there's a special police department for victims of violence like me so that I don't have to make tortuous multiple statements.

Annika suddenly realizes she's just got herself into a situation that has changed her face. She's leaning on the radiator, trembling on the overstrained floor and looking pitiable in a disgustingly sentimental way, which makes me feel aggressive and superior in equal measure.

Hyperventilating, I scream, 'You're so cruel, you only hit me on the head because my hair's so long and no one will see the bruises!'

Hyperventilating, Annika screams, 'Yeah, Jesus, fuck, what am I supposed to do?'

'Are you gonna ask me now how you ought to punish me for the whole thing? D'you want me to say, Hey, next time just ram a freaking Ikea lamp smack bang in my face!?'

'Oh God, just shut your bloody mouth, will you?'

'Aren't you scared I'll get a brain haemorrhage?'

'Mifti, you're not a bloody baby any more, only bloody babies have bloody brain haemorrhages!'

Hyperventilating, she gets up and staggers down the hall, hyperventilating. Just before she manages to escape to her room, our landline rings for the first time in six months. We look at each other, suddenly allied and utterly fazed. Completely knocked off our stride, we wait until the answer machine kicks in and the acoustic outcome of the vibration generated in our neighbour Lars's larynx casts a new light on our situation, making it look utterly ridiculous and inappropriate. Lars says, 'Yeah, hi, are any of you awake yet? I'm really bored, so I wanted to ask if I can come down for a minute and pick up my PlayStation. I lent Mifti my PlayStation three weeks ago. Bye bye then.'

Annika's just like, 'Is he crazy? It's eight in the morning!'

I apply mascara in front of the bathroom mirror, put on a turquoise silk kaftan dress that allegedly has something subtly impressive about it (whatever subtle may mean in this context), and say, 'Bye, Annika!'

An impassive Annika says, 'Are you going to school in a Halston dress that cost one and a half thousand dollars?'

* * *

I slam the front door behind me. Exhausted, I sit down on our doormat and summon up exactly where the problems lie.

1. I have absolutely no inclination to go to school right now.
2. I have a mother of a headache.
3. Our doormat is printed with the words *Yoga Mat* – and that's so out of order.
4. I urgently need to find a way to get back into the bastard flat.

You have a tendency to think up unnecessary to-do lists as an aid to spending the next twenty minutes outside the closed front door in a vaguely useful manner:

1. Music exists solely to preserve emotions. Karen Carpenter and Richard Carpenter.
2. Why does the sun go on shining? Why do the birds go on singing? Don't they know it's the end of the world?
3. Van Morrison, *Gloria*, continuing hyperventilation and the memory of the phrase, let out of the wall of Edmond's teeth, a few weeks ago: 'All I can do is run, run fast and run away and over and over again. Patti Smith's an old junkie – what is it with you and all these old women? Age doesn't make anyone any better. Ageing just means getting stale and jaded.'
4. Instead of wasting away in a state of anguish beyond all repair outside the front door, I simply open the door again.

Annika is sitting at the kitchen table along with her high-definition mascara and looking at me as if my thin-skinned nature has evolved into a now inconceivable unscrupulousness within a matter of moments.

'I don't have to go to school any more, Annika.'

'This is the end of the line.'

'Yeah, it really is the end. Everyone's unconscious outside.'

'I don't believe a word of it.'

'It doesn't matter if you believe me or not. Everyone outside's unconscious.'

She takes a paranoid look around.

'Nuclear war?'

'Chemical assault?'

'Close the window, Mifti.'

'Too late.'

Annika loses consciousness; I fall over. Both of us think we're the only one putting on a show. It's incredibly sexy.

Yes, we were all close to tears, and I have to admit it quite honestly, even though you don't get that very often with me, but if there are moments when you're close to tears, then this was certainly one of them, so we were all very close to tears.

At 8:10 a.m. Lars, his two-year-old brat and a superlative heap of expectation are standing in our hallway. The two-year-old brat is wearing a white crocheted Chilean poncho and has never had his freedom of choice restricted in the slightest and therefore grabbed a full pack of North Sea prawns out of our fridge within twenty seconds of his arrival and then gobbled down the content of said pack on the spot.

Lars spent three years studying graphic design in London. He's a vegan.

Intimacy

When our neighbour Lars was studying graphic design in London, he photographed shells from inside for a project with the set title of *Intimacy*, justifying this admittedly utterly crap idea by claiming that the interior of a shell had a great deal in common with the human anatomy and muscular structure. And all that.

Mifti (shocked): Pardon?

Lars: No, so I like justified it that a shell, from inside . . . I don't know exactly, there's something totally intimate about the structure of the interior of a shell.

Mifti: And you handed that in? That's really majorly shit!

Lars: The guy thought I was taking the piss as well, odd huh?

Mifti: You're a German vegan with over-sized ears – you can't hand in shells when you're studying graphic design in London.

Lars: What would you have handed in then?

Mifti: No idea, I'd probably have taken photos of movie stills from *Intimacy*.

Lars: No, be honest.

Mifti: I'd have photographed skin. I'd have handed in a whole 35-mm film of skin blemishes. Or intimate body piercings.

Lars: No, tell me honestly what you'd have handed in!

Mifti: Who got the most gushing praise for their project?

Lars: This Taiwanese girl who took photos of bleeding feet and a telephone and crap like that and some old posters hanging on walls. And she said she re-created peripheral settings, because the peripheral settings are like the thing that makes us remember intimate situations most incisively, so that's what she recreated.

Mifti: I'd have photographed pages from my grandma's photo album, where my mother stole photos of herself as a child. You can see the pages and the fact that something used to be there and that photos have been stolen, by my mother, pictures of my dead mother. Nobody knows where the photos are now. I don't think there's anything more intimate in the world.

The Social Lie

When I lie, I lie neurotically and compulsively. My lies result from a dependence on metaphysical occurrences. When Annika lies, her lies are supposed to make the person on the receiving end feel better or enhance the harmony of the group, or at least its motivation to achieve great things. She's firmly convinced of all that.

Lars: Yeah, I'm really sorry to bother you right now, but it's really crap with no PlayStation on a crappy day like today.

Mifti (*tossing her hair back with a cool gesture*): No worries, Lars! But I didn't manage to get through the game. I don't know, first I shot down six hundred zombies a minute, but the bad thing was that later this sea monster came along with this thing in its back, and I didn't hit it with the anchor.

Lars: It's not an anchor, it's a harpoon!

Mifti: I think it is an anchor, because the guy was just being spontaneous and he didn't have a harpoon handy on his rowing boat and then he tried to ram the anchor into the big fish's frontal extremities remodelled into fins, but then I just didn't quite manage it.

Lars: Probably because you have to set the dog free from the bear trap at the beginning and you didn't do it. When I got to that bit the dog helped me with the big fish because I saved him in the first level.

Mifti: That bastard dog? Shit!

Lars: Yeah, shit.

Mifti: What a crock of shit. What kind of shit is that anyway? You shoot down human beings with the B key held down, and then at the end of the day it's all a matter of some white Saint Bernard Greenland dog cross-breed.

Annika: What kind of alien dialogue are you two conducting here, kiddies?

Lars: Jesus, Mifti, turn around again a minute.

Mifti (*who has just accidentally turned the blood-soaked back of her head in Lars's direction for a brief moment to run into the kitchen and fetch him an empty mustard jar full of squash for him and the brat*): Annika beat me up.

Annika gives a bold, confident laugh, wiping the alarming sadistic tendencies escaped from her subconscious off the face of the earth. Nobody will ever accuse her of any such thing.

Lars: Hey, Mifti, that just sounded totally bad, you really shouldn't say that kind of thing in public, I bet someone might even believe it.

Mifti: Annika beat me up, Lars, I'm not kidding.

Lars: I mean it, Mifti, you mustn't say that sort of thing in public, you make it sound so plausible that everyone would believe it if they didn't know Annika.

Annika: It looks pretty heavy, huh? That's why we didn't pick up the phone before – Mifti didn't get out of bed as usual with her total lack of fucking discipline and then she did, and then she went out the door and came back again! Imagine that!

Lars: Are you crazy, Mifti?

Annika: Mifti?

Lars: Mifti?

Brat: Mifti?

Annika: And then after that Mifti kind of

suddenly banged her head on the junior
soldering iron Edmond keeps in his room.

Lars: What junior soldering iron?

Annika: The junior soldering iron that the
cocker spaniel Chantal dodged a couple of
months ago, and that meant Chantal caused
a car accident. Edmond bought the junior
soldering iron in an internet auction because
he thought the story to go with the junior
soldering iron was so awesome.

Lars (*concerned, to Mifti*): Why aren't you at
school today again? Why don't you just get
down to it?

And then Mifti sets fire to Berlin-Mitte. She strangles
Lars to death with a telephone wire, throws the
two-year-old brat unpretentiously out of a third-floor
window and gives Annika a seeing-to with an iron prop
the size of her hand, equipped with sharp tines for the
purpose of first tearing to shreds the flesh of its victim
hanging by their arms and then scraping the flesh down
to their bones. And then Mifti goes to visit Alice, who's
lying on her roof terrace with a distinct lack of interest
and a joint in her hand. Mifti ties Alice to a table and
places a cage on her chest, containing a rat. As there are
glowing coals on top of the cage, the rat attempts to
gnaw its way out through the victim.

By now we're sitting at the breakfast table. Annika
washes down half a Ritalin with low-fat chocolate milk
and divides the contents of the second pack of North Sea
prawns into three equal portions. Lars, Annika and I are
getting on like a house on fire.

Annika asks, 'What would you have had at school today then?'

'Huh?'

'You know, what subjects? What classes are you missing? Maths? If you miss technical drawing again you'll fail!'

'They're all going to some concentration camp today.'

'Fantastic!'

Anyone from the seventies here? Let's talk
(Leisha Hailey)

I'm currently on a suburban railway platform, and I'm not under the influence of drugs on this occasion. Instead, I'm standing at the ticket machines in the company of two sixteen-year-old female classmates from Berlin's most affluent area. The two of them are wearing neon headbands with fleece linings, and I'm not an outcast, pseudo-arrogant compulsive truant. Instead, I'm a quiet, integrated member of a class of twenty-seven adolescents constantly attempting to impress one another. The difference between them and me is that I don't feel the need to make anything of myself, that there are photos of me as a child which prompt no other reaction than, great, far too much wisdom in such a small face. My teachers don't know the meaning of the term 'ambiguity tolerance'. They just know intuitively that it's a pretty big deal to be nice to me right now, so in other words, they do know it.

Margit Kratzmüller says, 'Hey, cool, you're back. Where've you been?'

'I had secondary pneumonia and had to have antiviral therapy every morning.'

'Woah, we really missed you.'

'Yeah, wicked.'

'I've got a boyfriend now.'

'Great, how old is he?'

'Uh, eighteen?'

'Anyone I know?'

'He's a friend of the flatmate of that model I had a thing with.'

'That bastard of a model off Facebook with the Billabong top?'

'That's the one, only he's not on Facebook any more, and I always thought, if he's not on Facebook any more he must be dead.'

'Probably is.'

'Yeah, I bet. Anyway, we were right up the top of this club on Alexanderplatz, and I kind of scraped all the skin off my back.'

'So you had sex with this guy on the staircase at Weekend and you scraped all the skin off your back?'

'Yeah, and you?'

I bury my face in my arms. 'I'm not the talking-about-it type.'

'Oh yeah, you and your issues with genitals.'

'What?'

'You told me about it one time, remember? About your issues with genitals.'

'I have issues with sex, because sex counteracts unconditional love, and that's what I want. Sex is nothing but a selfish, bestial urge that unmasks the people I love as remote-controlled conglomerations of reflexes. Actually you're right, I do have issues with genitals. *Imagine la scène suivante . . .*'

'What does that mean?'

'Picture the following scene: you're sitting on the red armchair in your room, and your new, eighteen-year-old boyfriend places a book with the most complicated, philosophical problem complexes in your hands, which he wants you to structure systematically for him. Let's say Giorgio Agamben's *Homo Sacer*.'

'OK.'

'You think nothing of it and you start reading out some text about the juridical schism of your identity into a socialized entity, containing words like "abrogated", I mean really heavy stuff, and suddenly he starts fingering you. You want to toss the book aside and enjoy but he forces you to read the text to the end.'

'Yeah . . .'

'Anyway, after three syllables at most, the whole thing develops into an incredible struggle between your body and your mind. Between biology and intellect. You try really hard to carry on making some kind of rational sense out of what you're reading, but at some point you just can't because your muscles and your hormones are resisting like crazy. And at some point you come, and you drop the book. Your body, which doesn't actually have anything to do with you, has won out over you. Some people say that's absolute gratification. But for me it's just frightening.'

'Then you're scared of losing control.'

'No, I wouldn't say that.'

'Well, all the stuff you say always sounds very clever, anyway.'

'Thanks.'

'Jürgen?'

'Good thing you're ringing, Mifti. I was just about to go and puke.'

'What?'

'I can't do it now, can I?'

'Why were you going to puke?'

'Anorexic attack. But anyway, as I said, I just won't puke now.'

'Are you on your own? Did you get my masochism text?'

'Yes. Where are you right now?'

'At a concentration camp. It's just not imparting any kind of vision. Our twenty-seven-strong class is evenly spread across a semi-circular parade ground that used to be closed in by four barracks ordered in a fan shape.'

'Are you in Sachsenhausen? I puked outside the sickbay there once.'

'Instead of puking outside the sickbay, I've just been chatting about a loose contact in my audio guide, so to speak. How was your day?'

'Peeing scenes in a multi-storey car park where we didn't have permission to film.'

'Can you get me out of here?'

'Mifti?'

'When are we going to see each other?'

'Day after tomorrow? At Albrecht and Samatha's wedding – you are invited, aren't you? Oh, I meant to say, don't worry too much about why you made Annika beat you up. All that masochist crap gets less and less of a deal as it goes on. In ten years you'll be having perfectly normal legal sex, with equal rights based on mutual love. With people who aren't members of your family.'

'You said that in a really lovely way, Jürgen, but I suspect it's a huge pile of crap.'

'At some point you'll be a really hard-boiled sadist. At some point you'll even realize that genitals can be beautiful. Don't you ever feel like clamping clothes pegs on the nipples of your entire drainpipe-jeans-clad class and then twisting them?'

'No. They're all too cute.'

'Cute is silver, but sadism is golden.'

'I trod on a snail outside Berghain the other day.'

'Ha ha.'

'Yeah, I got the shock of my life. It was awful, even just the crushing sound and then that weird girl Hersilie, do you know her? Anyway, she goes—'

'D'you mean Hersilie with that badass "I'm playing a prostitute in a movie" look?'

'That's the one. Anyway, she's like, "Now you know what you're going to be in your next life, a snail outside Berghain."'

'OK. You can use that later in life, in your Buddhist phase on some beach in Thailand when everyone's talking about reincarnation and saying, "Hey, I'd like to come back as a tree" or "I want to be reincarnated as a leaf", and you just give this mega-disillusioned shout, "I know what I'm going to be – a snail outside Berghain."'

'Shit.'

'So where does it go, your soul?'

'Either to heaven or to hell. Or it turns into a butterfly.'

There are so many years of my life I spent in a kind of rigor mortis or whatever you call it, frozen like a rabbit in the headlights, so like not moving because, you know, this can't really be life, can it, and you have to just get through it, that terrible time, you have to go through what other people dictate are necessary experiences, but they make you think: I'm not actually the slightest bit interested. What am I writing here?

* * *

The first day at my new school was approximately eight months ago.

I enter a building that I've finally tracked down in the middle of a patch of woodland, following a fifty-six-minute train journey. From now on I will answer every inquiry on my family background with, 'I don't have a family.' I swear that to myself after my first two steps on the speckled blue laminate floor covering, which requests in an unacceptable tone that I bid farewell to my existence as a combat bitch from hell discussing intellectual trends on auspicious late-summer evenings. I think, 'Apartment, wrestling, rock 'n' roll.' Every metre robs me of part of my vocabulary. I won't be capable of anything in this place in the near future, apart from permanently forgetting to fold my worksheets in the middle before I punch holes to file them. If you don't punch holes in worksheets at the right place, they end up sticking out of the ring binder in an ugly untidy manner and earning you a less than gratifying grade for 'reliability and conscientiousness' in your end-of-year report.

And then at some point I just stopped turning up, so to speak. Not because I think people can do without education; it was because I just couldn't deal with it. That kind of thing's never a conscious decision, it's an act of desperation. I just found the unserious side of life much better, that sexy moment, the provisional, the luxurious and the playful elements. The fact that it makes no sense at all to be alive. And that it's an absolute cheek that you have to die. I often fall asleep thinking these thoughts. I feel like life's majorly taking the piss, because my consciousness will automatically end up pushing up daisies when my body stops working, even though I actually . . .

It's 12:30 p.m. I find everything Herr Kroschinske is saying interesting.

Herr Kroschinske: 'In that building over there are tiny dungeons where people were locked away in the dark for months on end.'

I light a cigarette.

'That's not such a good idea, Mifti.'

'Sorry.'

I put my cigarette out again and put on the credible smile of a person willing to make a sacrifice. Herr Kroschinske puts on a credible calm smile back. A boy from a different class, whose name I don't know, yells, 'FUCK, WHY AREN'T WE ALLOWED TO SMOKE HERE? THERE'S SHITLOADS OF BUTTS IN THAT BIN THERE!'

'Anatol Schmidt, the problem is, I talked to the people here when we arrived and smoking is just not allowed here.'

'Jesus, but I mean, there's loads of fag ends in this bin, for fuck's sake!'

'That's presumably because other people have ignored the no-smoking rule and then somebody collected up all their butts and threw them in the bin later, I've no idea, and why are you taking your cigarettes out so demonstratively?'

'WHAT? WE'RE NOT ALLOWED TO SMOKE HERE?'

'No, you're not allowed to smoke here.'

'Jesus, shit, what are we gonna do now?'

'Well, we can decide in a moment if we want to leave the premises as a group, but first of all can you all have another look at the white lines over here, there was a building over there where six hundred people were deliberately assassinated because they were regarded as biologically inferior, and they really all died.'

The class leaves the premises as a group even before Herr Kroschinske has finished his sentence. On the way I talk crap to Virginia, who's wearing four pairs of tights at once.

'And one time, Mifti, I sent my father a text and it said, "Fear Dad." And he like texts me back, "Dear Virginia, I assume you meant DEAR Dad? Have you got a problem with your T9?"'

'What an anus.' (I find it so difficult to exercise full concentration because it seems so incredibly old-fashioned, etc.)

So this is the funeral I've always wished for, right? My father, my mother, my child and my brother and sister and my grandparents are all dead. Because my family's been wiped out, I've suddenly become a discount funeral parlour for some inexplicable reason, in which the lower middle class dies after it's dead. Everything's real but there are times real is fake, flowers, tons of smells, wood halls polished like fingernails. I'm struggling through a mass of poorly dressed people all staring at me – I don't allow anyone uglier than me to watch me crying or collapsing to the floor under the pressure of this widely spread standard definition of authenticity – and attempting to maintain the appearance of a cathartic effect in a credibly obnoxious manner.

I want to inherit four hundred shares and I've just calculated how hysterical I am when the preacher asks me, 'Do you know anything good for me to say (I have to say something: SAY SOMETHING!) over your family's mutilating bodies?' And I tell him how beautiful they all were. No one cries, they're all there to stare at me. Did I really love them? I want a pet that can turn round in circles. The head teacher Frau Pegler shouts down the telephone, 'Mifti, I consider you the most immoral person I've ever come across.'

I refuse to let this two-bit whore turn me into a lobotomy case.

'What?'

'I consider you the most immoral person I've ever come across, and I insist right now, at this very moment, regardless of whether a huge stone just fell on your head two seconds ago or not, I insist that you get right on a train this instant and appear in my office in less than two hours from now.'

'All right.'

'All right?'

'Frau Pegler, you know perfectly well I'm not capable of making it easy for you to build up any form of trust in me.'

Herr Kroschinske brushes a bushel of hair out of his face with an unnaturally unstrained gesture, looking elsewhere and then kind of back at me again after all. While he's still resisting the impulse not to take the side of a totally and utterly neurotic head teacher this time around, instead taking that of a problem child pretending to be fully reflective of herself and therefore unassailable, I hang up. I hand him back his mobile phone, imparting five different impressions through a single cool gesture: I am expected to get on my bike a.s.a.p., Frau Pegler is an insecure cunt whose misguided educational methods are inappropriate but understandable, you're a really cool teacher and I totally like you, your hair's pretty cool as well, I'll fill in that really interesting worksheet you put together and handed out before we arrived at the concentration camp at home and present it to the whole class the year after next as part of the presentation I'll have to give to make up for missing three hundred days of school in the months to come. Thank you for being pleased to see me.

The train I find myself on twenty minutes later is named after the former chancellor Helmut Schmidt.

I attempt to elevate my basic mood to that of the past year. A state of such productive sentimentality that I had no other option but to dance to techno mixes of violin passages in front of the mirror with lead weights around my ankles. Every track was a personal challenge. I'd have swallowed electricity if it had enabled me to spend longer than forty-eight hours leaping ecstatically around a puke-encrusted dance floor. A period when strangers on trains whispered, 'Crazy choreography', rather than ignoring me, a period dominated by an idea raised above any will to survive: the idea that Alice and I had of one another – an answer to all questions, which lay in the absolute intensity of my desire, a desire impossible to translate into a specific demand.

It doesn't work. Nor does looking out of the window. Nor does imagining you're driving a Vespa across the ground floor of a mid-range department store, whacked on a weekday afternoon and categorizing the soft golden flashes of the watch display cases as an adequate replacement for everything you've had taken away from you over the past two years: dreams, desires, sexuality, faith. An underworld in a land that's menstruating, turning to shit day after day and plunging all the existences patched together out of fantasies to their doom with its relentless putrefaction: they all die.

They play, eat, fuck, sleep, wake up, forget to be in when the gas man comes, they order inflatable gymnastic balls to strengthen their back muscles, download Iggy Pop's discography for free, finish their vocational training as landscape gardeners, make a wrong decision, book a package holiday, spend a year on an exchange living with Mormons in Las Vegas, decorate their flat to go with the season, get themselves a four-legged friend whose excrements have to be stored temporarily in plastic bags and then thrown away, split up, call their school band 'Planet Palin', become grandparents, are severely impressed, have bad skin, get stabbed, lose their left leg in a car accident, buy buttermilk, respond to the question of their star sign with the word, 'Arsehole', set up the website www.live-rapes.com, and have been wondering for years why mattress stores are always on street corners.

Frau Pegler holds up a piece of paper in front of my face, on which her secretary has written in her best hand-writing: 'Mifti will be ten minutes late.'

She waves it around under my nose in all seriousness for thirty seconds. I start to suspect my head teacher might be mentally disabled.

'I just found this on my desk.'

'I called to say the train was running late.'

'The fact is that you didn't do everything in your capacity to get here on time.'

I smile at Frau Pegler and allow her to place me on a dark blue upholstered chair, which would be reason enough in my sister's view to leave the office instantly. With the aid of a final spark of self-discipline and the thought of a serene green meadow, I manage to keep my aggression in check and my gob modestly shut.

'Mifti, I have a hundred and fifty per cent instinct for good and evil. And you are definitely evil.'

'Are your thirteen years of experience with psychologically unstable adolescents not enough to tell you that that statement's going to push me over the edge into a big fat identity crisis?'

'No.'

'Do you really mean that seriously? Do we really have to have this conversation on this level?'

'Yes.'

'Frau Pegler, somebody's just trying to criticize the hell out of you in a stylish and appropriate manner, and all you can do is say yes and no.'

No answer from Frau Pegler.

'Someone's criticizing you to hell in a stylish and appropriate manner, and what do you do? You don't say ANYTHING. What a crock of shit!'

I wish someone would ask me how my day went at school.

I got the elation, hesitation, dissipation, coagulatin',
relaxation, angxation, emancipation, propagation,
moppin', soppin', talkin' 'bout your coppin' blues
(The Charlatans)

Funnily enough, it's pretty simple. The incredible paean
to a well-planned lighting concept, which only a few
seconds ago consisted of nothing more than two misplaced floor lamps. A kebab shop turning more and
more into the desired techno palace with every blink. The
question of whether a life spent sober can ever have any
point.

Edmond, having stuffed a Turkish börek in his mouth
while mumbling that he really ought to get more poetic,
provides the answer to this all-important question: 'And
at last it's all over, our hearts are really pretty fucked, but
suddenly they're not scared any more of turning into
historical documents!'

Yeah, right. I'm wearing a dark blue parka, and the
present day is still burning through the material into my
back muscles. The world is melting. When I glance at my
wrist, three stamps remind me that Berlin belongs to me.
Varnished wooden furniture with unacceptably pat-
terned upholstery, the walls decorated with enlarged
passport photos of the children of the man currently
standing behind a glass counter, with a daily habit of

103

processing salmonella-infected meat using high-quality kebab slicing equipment.

I say, 'You guys have got it so good, you've got siblings.'

Instead of diverting her attention to me, Annika leans over the back of her chair, her eyes closed. I'm vulnerable in this respect.

She says, 'Don't talk such a load of crap, you've got siblings too. You've got us – we're incompetent and crap, but we're your brother and sister.'

'That's not what I mean – you grew up together and everything.'

'We shared bunk beds.'

'Exactly.'

'That was completely shit, it's nothing to envy.'

'But what you said the other day sounded so awesome, when you were staying in that holiday home with Dad in Zurich and you decided you wanted to eat fish, but then his girlfriend wanted to buy this cheap salmon at the supermarket and you said, "No, we're getting proper fish!" And then the stupid cunt dragged Dad down to the basement and shrieked, "I can't take it, this whole luxury crap and all the whole crap and they're so spoilt and all that – they get it from their mother."'

'Jesus, I'd almost repressed that memory.'

'And then you looked at Edmond and asked if you ought to call up the car-sharing agency and get a lift home, and Edmond like pursed his lips and nodded.'

Edmond, 'Did you tell her that, Annika? That I pursed my lips and nodded?'

'Anyway, I thought it was so great that you weren't alone. Imagine if it'd been me sitting there, I couldn't have looked at anyone to make sure it wasn't me that was the problem, it was that stupid cunt's inadequate reaction that was the problem.'

'Please stop saying stupid cunt, I'll pick it up and if those words come out of my mouth at the agency tomorrow morning, some intern in snakeskin boots will ask if I have Tourette's syndrome.'

'But don't you understand what I mean?'

'The thing is though, while you were at the concentration camp yesterday, Edmond admitted that he fed my hazelnut-brown mouse to the cat.'

Edmond sniggers.

'I went crazy, Mifti.'

'What hazelnut-brown mouse?'

'We used to have two mice each, I had two girl mice and Edmond had two boys. And at some point we thought it'd be like really cool to swap one of them over, and suddenly we both had twenty mice each, and they were all black or white or kind of spotted. But I had a tiny hazelnut-brown mouse in my litter, and it was the total freak in the family and it always did different stuff. It was just a really cool mouse, and one day it just disappeared.'

'It always did different stuff?'

'Yeah, really, like if the others were digging like tunnels inside their little hutch, she'd sit down on the roof and do nothing.'

'And then?'

'All of a sudden she disappeared. I looked for her everywhere. In the garden, everywhere, in the fridge, I swear, and then at first I thought she'd just run away, but she really couldn't have got out of the little hutch, you'd never have managed it as a mouse. I checked everywhere, but the bastard mouse just wasn't there any more.

And while you were at the concentration camp yester day Edmond suddenly piped up, "Annika, I have to tell you something, no actually, oh God, maybe I'll wait another year." And I'm like, "Hey, come on, just tell me right now," and he's like, "I fed your hazelnut-brown mouse to the cat."' Annika lets out a deep breath, as if she expected a compliment for not killing Edmond.

'Man, Annika, I'm really sorry, Jesus.'

I'm like, 'Why didn't you kill him when he admitted it?'

'I was just sad. And then he told me in all this detail how the cat played around with the mouse, and then I thought, maybe at the beginning the mouse was still – oh no, really, that can't be true.'

Edmond, 'It was no fun for the mouse, Annika.'

'No, I don't think it was.'

'Me neither, Mifti.'

'And what else happened back then?'

'Edmond always slept on the top bunk, and this one afternoon he was sitting up there in the middle of some hyperactive phase, our mother wasn't in, and suddenly he goes, "Hey, Annika, I'm gonna pretend I'm a figurehead." And I'm like, "You're so disturbed, kid!" And then he went right ahead and leaned right over and then he fell out of the top bunk on his head, and guess what I did next, Mifti.'

'No idea.'

'I wrapped all this toilet paper round his head because it was bleeding like crazy.'

'How old were you?'

'Dunno, six and nine or something?'

Naturally enough, none of the three of us want to

come into contact with any kind of unsettling everyday life ever again.

Text from Ophelia to Mifti, who is standing in front of a mirror looking at herself as if she had to make out not herself but a huge crowd of people: 'Mifti, I maltreated my lower arms dispassionately with a bread knife and now I wish I could run away. I wish I could run away. I can't take it any more.'

While I look at myself in this disappointing way for minutes on end, I think I can feel the beginning of a smile. My hair is stuck to my forehead, my skin is more semi-gloss than ever for some inexplicable reason, and I count my eyelashes. The effect of my reflected self hits me directly with the suddenness of an arrow, beginning to bore through me in my most distant memories: a pain that's none other than my own.

The only thing still visible is the unbounded weakness and the resulting innocence. Not taking my eyes off myself, I try to remind myself that the skin above the backs of my knees, the scar tissue between my shoulders and the field of freckles on one thigh are all part of me.

I squeeze through a small window into the dark backyard, from which the Rammstein album echoing out of the kebab shop is driving out a leap of leopards. My brother and sister won't think to investigate my whereabouts, they're too busy distinguishing effects and side effects from one another. All I know is that I love myself and that I love every one of my steps, I'm trembling so much, no idea why, that I can only walk about five yards, and then I sit down on the kerb to flag down a taxi at some point.

I say, 'OK, I have absolutely no idea where I want to go.'

'Are you excited?'

'Why are you asking me that?'

'You look like you're just about to meet someone you're in love with.'

'But I just said I have no idea where I want to go.'

The taxi driver drives off, watching me in the mirror as I take off my parka. I write my name on the steamed-up window with one finger, and the words, 'Yesterday I had the most terrible dream. I dreamed I was a plastic bag.'

'So what does that mean – you've got no idea where you want to go?'

'OK, let's go home.'

'You've just been smoking, haven't you?'

'Is that some kind of problem?'

'No, I'm not one of those militant anti-smokers. But I gave up before you were even born, I should think. I've been a non-smoking taxi ever since.'

'So you've been a non-smoking taxi ever since.'

'I even threw someone out the other day.'

'For smoking?'

'No, he got in and he'd especially ordered a non-smoking taxi, and then he wanted to look in the ashtray to make absolutely sure there was no smoking in here. And I said, "No, get out. That's beyond the pale, really."'

'Funny.'

'Yeah. I've only ever let one passenger smoke in here. He was standing there and he'd just lit up a Havana. I

108

pulled up and he says, "Oh, I forgot to order a smoking taxi." And I said, "Herr Müller, no problem, go ahead and get in." Then we wound down all the windows and we drove down Oranienburger Strasse at five miles an hour at the most, and whenever someone gave us a look, we waved at them like that sheikh, what's his name again?'

'That was very nice of you.'

'Yes, I mean, Heiner Müller, you've probably never heard of him, but in a situation like that you just have to—'

'*The* Heiner Müller? The playwright?'

'Heiner Müller.'

We drive through Mitte by night. When he stops the car I realize I haven't got any money left and I ask if he wants me to leave my ID card but he answers, 'No, I trust you,' and I run upstairs to the darkened flat, where all I can find is a 500 euro note that he can't change, so we drive to a cashpoint, I give him his stupid thirteen euro fare, and he says, 'Get back in again, at the front, I'll drive you back.'

He doesn't give me a second glance until he stops the car in the empty car park of an exhibition space for designer furniture reached via a spiral ramp, and gets out. I wind down the window to give him my half-smoked cigarette, cold hitting me with an above average unpleasant bite. Disgust, pure lechery, egoism, a farewell to all intellectual fads and to the romantic idea of a life-affirming night out.

He tugs my head up, I can't remember how I got rid of my underwear, I have a dark red, wrinkly penis in my face and I'm watching its owner as the beastly bastard fucks his way rhythmically through the situation, lunging with his extenuated hairy balls all over all the body parts I made out as my own less than an hour ago. He sticks his index finger in my mouth and attempts to look like Enrique Iglesias in the video for *Hero*. His dribbling tongue licks my rib cage in such an uncivilized manner that his saliva gland secretions seem to drip off my skin by the litre on to the beige leather seats. I prop myself up to arch my back, thereby pressing my torso into his face, which by now is twitching uncontrollably out of lechery. Somehow, the two of us entirely independently existing individuals continue along this road as if we were a single entity, until we stop, and at this point of pause for thought he says, completely out of breath after trying to stick something or other down my throat again, I don't know whether it was membrane-enclosed muscle or his shin or his dick, 'Are you an actress?'

'How do you know?'

'I'm a radio presenter. You have such clean diction, you have that characteristic actor's style, I knew all along you were an actress.'

'Why are you driving a taxi then?'

'They took my show off the air.'

So then I decide out of the blue not to make any appearance any more. I know he's fucking my brains out – I don't want this indecent knowledge, it means losing my language; I have no language in this world of pure sex. Nothing about it is disgusting or interspersed with explosions of ecstasy or revolting. The most unsavoury thing is that my body comes several times over, shaken by multiple orgasms during the course of these three rounds of strenuous procedure. No sexual tension released via involuntary muscle contractions, no high and no liberation. Just a seemingly never-ending spiral of overpowerment through piles and piles of feelings, dominated by pity and the contours finally traceable again after my traumatic odyssey through the world of psychedelic mind expansion. The sobriety returning. The thought of my grandmother calling to tell me that dandelions were her daughter's favourite flowers – her dead daughter, even though children aren't supposed to die before their parents. Anyway, children dying, that's crazy.

My grandad, secretly going to a playground in his cord hat to play on the swing with his eyes closed. The money I saved up to buy my teddy a little school satchel made of red leather.

The taxi driver climbs awkwardly over the seats back to the steering wheel and starts the car. I start my third pack of cigarettes. I try to work out what order I should go through all the addresses that might come into question as destinations to tell him. Actually, the question isn't the number or the order of various addresses to choose from. The only question is whether Ophelia is still alive.

'I have to go to my father's place. You can just let me out anywhere you like, it's up to you. I have to run through town until I fall unconscious in a puddle of petrol with a torn diaphragm, incapable of anything more than hoping someone accidentally throws a match into the puddle. And while I'm lying there I'll listen to this really clever playlist I put together with totally obscure unknown songs by these sixties garage bands from American small towns, there's this site on the net where you can download them, and at the same time you download a real feeling of exclusivity because you think nobody except you has ever listened to them. Like there's this one song called "Loving You Sometimes". I listened to it and thought, shit, shit, there must be some way to express what I feel for this damn song that's just reeled out of some genius musician's heart straight into my arms. And then I realized, I can't express it, because I haven't got any weapons of expression any more, all I have is an input capacity glowering over my existence that can't be switched off and has transformed my entire mental life into tangled strings of sausages. I'm a tangled string of sausages. I'm probably not going to survive the whole thing. Just chuck me out anywhere, all right?'

'OK, but can I just ask you if you're kind of disturbed in any way?'

'What?'

'You're talking nine to the dozen here about strings and sausages, you're really kinda weird – did you take a single breath just now?'

'Have you got some kind of a problem?'

'No, have you?'

'I haven't got a problem, you've got a problem.'

'Now you pipe down. It's about time you realized it's definitely not me who's got a problem here.'

'I haven't got a problem, you mong!'

'Well, nice to have talked about it.'

'I'm underage.'

'I hate that, all you underage girls who imagine I'm going to shack up with you in some holiday home or something.'

'Twenty-six-year-olds are worse. They want to go the whole hog.'

112

'Whole hogs are no problem at all.'

'Why not?'

'All that means is that someone keeps the fridge stocked up, you share an Ikea bed and pretend you're not in when the gas man comes round. All the rest is just unrealistic fantasy crap that holds you back and blocks you and disappoints you and gets on your nerves. I've only got this one life and I'm never gonna see the inside of a holiday home, and that's actually completely acceptable in view of the fact that we're all going to die anyway and then we won't even remember that study trip to Uzbekistan or that holiday home on the Baltic coast. All everyone ever wants is to experience something or other. Everyone wants to spend six months of their lives in Tanzania or eat cockroaches up a tree in Burkina Faso.'

'Or build a children's home in Afghanistan.'

'Right. Any day now I'm going to wantonly shoot fifty holes in some random person's lungs, just so I can spend the rest of my life in jail and finally don't have to be part of this society any more, where you're not obliged to do anything except take constant responsibility for your own reputation.'

'Would you really kill someone to go to prison?'

'No, I don't think so. I might steal a car or rob a perfumery or chuck a stone through a window and then let myself get caught.'

'I could go to the police and say you raped me if you like.'

'I might get back to you on that one.'

'It's a fantastic plan. I can spend the rest of my life legitimizing everything I do wrong with some rape, and you get banged up for four years.'

'Four years of TV, plenty to eat and basketball on the weekend.'

'Sounds great.'

'If you like that kind of thing.'

I say my goodbyes and get out of the car. I look round one single time; the taxi's still there and the guy gives a slightly embarrassed wave from the distance.

Hot tar rains down from the star-spangled sky, reminding me I've arrived on the lowest level of disillusionment and have no chance of a salutary turn to excess opening up before my feet. I'm too disillusioned to look for positive side effects in the depths of my self-pity. Not even self-pity is an option any more. I can neither run nor put on my headphones. The worst thing is, I can't cry. We human beings actually only cry when we're happy, because there's nothing more dangerous for our hearts than dust.

Dust is the only dirt that can do us any harm.

My fear's so huge that I can't even breathe any more. I'm walking through a part of town full of individuals in neat and tidy outfits, all sufficiently trusting and socially competent to distract one another from their sobering knowledge of the pointlessness of human existence. Me and my amphetamine-ridden repulsion wait more than twenty minutes outside the bastard of an eggshell-white building I want to enter, until some fashionista faggot opens the door to me from inside. He wraps a scarf around his neck as he steps outside and I squeeze past him into the entrance. He presumably thinks I must be homeless and says to himself, hmmm. Once I've dashed down a corridor still filthy with unfinished concrete repair work, I discover an extremely misplaced-looking rubber plant in a pot on the third floor. With hectic paws, I shovel most of the earth out of it and come across the spare key, which I plan to use to break into my father's flat. Logically enough, he didn't tell me to my face that he'd buried a spare key under the rubber plant on the third floor; he yelled it at the current love of his life during some phone call, presumably while she was putting something through a juicer or flicking through a biography of Luis Buñuel. The phone call went something like this:

'Hello, Mifti!'

'Hello, Dad.'

'I just wanted to ask what you think about me giving Annika one of those funny cacti for her birthday, you know, the ones you attach to your mobile phone and then they get really huge.'

'What?'

'Haven't you ever seen a cell-phone cactus?'

'No.'

'Oh, right. My girlfriend Franziska says it's a great idea.'

'How is she, by the way?'

'She's fine, the only thing is I had this really long tortured conversation with this assistant woman last night about emotional depths that some up-and-coming actresses failed to capture in these Tibetan art-house films. And then I was so bored I made us all figs in Parma ham, and Franziska ate them too but then she went off, I mean to bed, I mean without me, I didn't go to bed until much later. And then this morning she came drooping out of the bathroom all sad and said she'd really wished she could be alone with me.'

'Jesus, Dad, you always have girlfriends who really wish for stuff, and then you keep on saying, "Yeah, my girlfriend Franziska really wished she could be alone with me" or "My girlfriend Jane really wished for a bit of humidity".'

'And how's things your end? I thought I'd take the opportunity to ask you!'

'Great.'

'I'm flying to Tokyo tomorrow, have I told you that?'

'Yes.'

'Isn't that awesome?'

'Yes.'

'Wouldn't you like to go to Tokyo some time?'

'No.'

'What?'

'I'm just such a bad tourist. Being a tourist would get me completely depressed, Dad, I'd just want to commit suicide. I can't do Asia. I don't want to revel in other people's misery. Italy, two thousand years of tourism, I could probably deal with that, but real travelling and looking at stuff and the mysteries of Laos and Cambodia – no thanks.'

'Have you ever even been on a plane?'

'No.'

'Seriously? You've never been abroad?'

'Nope. Actually yes, to France, to the coast or whatever it's called.'

'Shall I bring you a souvenir?'

'A Japanese baby.'

'Don't you want to start with a little puppy dog?'

'I wouldn't say no to a little puppy dog for my birthday.'

'Love you.'

'What?'

'Sorry, hold on a mo – FRANZISKA, I'M JUST BURYING ANOTHER SPARE KEY IN THE RUBBER PLANT POT, OK?'

The moment I enter the flat, everything my father bought for himself while my mother was spending her available funds on cheap plonk is splayed before my eyes. An original Leni Riefenstahl photo, a plasma screen, Indian wall hangings that look like someone brought them back from a wildlife safari, and a seventy-three-euro salt cellar. Tiny state-of-the-art remote controlled planes with a total value in the five figure range. All his favourite leisure devices, all his art, all his music. I steal a three-foot-high pile of Kinks records. On the topmost cover, he's stuck women's mouths cut out of porn mags, sperm running out of some of them.

I steal 2,000 euros. An unanticipated crashing rings out in my head. My systems are built on logic, analogies principally, contained within a concept. Yet as soon as I have no idea of the concept, the analogies become a jaded collection of out-of-context photographs that don't tell a story any more. When my hair blocks my view I notice that my hair colour is dark brown. That makes sense. Had gravity been abolished within the past twenty minutes it wouldn't have surprised me in the least. In fact I tip the entire contents of a bottle of vodka on to the worktop integrated into the dome-shaped kitchen system, for the sole purpose of getting worked up about the liquid not flowing upwards. If one and one is no longer two, shouldn't the world be coming to an end?

By the time I walk into the bedroom, see my father lying on his visco-elastic mattress and think at every breath that it might be my or his last, it's all too late. Every observation I've made over the past few hours contradicts the immediately plausible principle on which the certainty of my existence is based. It wouldn't have a single qualm about waking him.

Adaptation, I think, adaptation's what's needed here.

Why haven't I actually done anything at all over the past ten days? Oh yeah, I was unconscious.

2:15 a.m. Seeing as I could theoretically be asleep right now at home or at Ophelia's place or in the traditionally individualistically decorated apartment of some acquaintance collapsing under the burden of his or her personal misery, I abandon the idea of ringing Alice's doorbell. I squat down on my jacket in the backyard of her house, wedged into the gap between the regular and the recycling bin, strip down to my underwear and attempt a spot of unimpassioned freezing to death, or at least to get myself a series of impressive chilblains, or at the very least to pretend I have some kind of auto-aggressive complex on a worrying scale.

The last time I was homeless was when I was ten. I called my mother from a phone box and she didn't answer. It was the middle of summer. Individuals outlined as black silhouettes in short H&M sports clothing against a deep blue evening sky as they left the outdoor pool. My entire day consisted of the attempt to distract myself from the thought that she'd accidentally bled to death after biting off her own tongue.

We lived on the upper floor of a two-storey concrete prefab building, next door to a sixty-four-year-old deaconess who was convinced that war was God's explicit will to cleanse the world. There'd been a nursery on the ground floor but it had been closed down because of a fungus infestation. I climbed over the broken garden gate, which three years later was to prompt two acne-infested ambulance workers to break into a snide conversation about benefits scroungers instead of getting my half-dead mother out of our freaking flat as quickly as possible. It took six paces to the front door, which sent my fear right off the scale. I rang the doorbell; she didn't open up. Just like the day before. I rang at least twenty-two times at regular intervals before becoming firmly convinced she was dead. Then I ran off to some other phone box, and when I stopped and dialled my father's number, I noticed every breath of exhaustion coupled with panic felt as if it would tear my entire torso in two.

'Hello, Dad, this is Mifti I hope you listen to this message please get straight on a train and come here wherever you are Mum's dead she's not opening the door and I don't know what to do I just really don't know what to do now. And thanks for the armbands by the way.'

I ran back again. There was a narrow, overgrown garden behind our house. From there, I tried to smash one of our windowpanes with a stone. It didn't work. Despite its malnourished state of weakness, my four-foot-five body tried out all the options open to it, in a completely uncontrolled manner. I wept bitterly, threw flower boxes around the garden and spent at least half an hour running from one side of the garden to the other and then back to the first side and then to the other again. My last attempt consisted of leaning a seven-rung household ladder against the wall and leaping from the

top rung to the guttering, in the hope of pulling myself up on
to the flat roof. I dangled from the guttering for ten seconds.

1

2

3

4

5

6

7

8

9

10

Then I slipped off and landed in a semi-split on the rusted
remains of a broken barbecue. A sound emanated from
my left thigh, rather like someone biting into an apple
through a megaphone. The sound was so loud that it was
that that shocked me and not the pain that shot through
my pelvic area half a second later. When I tried to get up
I fell over. I scrabbled across the ground for a couple of
yards and then decided to stay lying there for the rest
of my life. I imagined how liberating it might be never
to have to love anyone ever again. I imagined living

in a little patch of woods next to the railway tracks after my mother's funeral, existing on blackberries and abandoned drink cans. Then I made the greatest mistake in my life to that date.

Someone called out: 'Mifti?'

I thought it was my mother, so I shouted, 'I'm here.'

Suddenly a bespectacled woman spilling out of her overly tight clothes and sporting a short black haircut was standing in front of me, at that moment seemingly the ugliest person I had ever seen. When I recognized her as the single parent of my classmate Charlene Kaplitz-Pittkowski, I leapt up, despite the pain, tidying my hair as a reflex.

'Your father called me.'

'What?'

She was a chemistry teacher and she'd been furious at me for months after I'd given Charlene's seven-year-old brother a Lara Croft beach towel, which she regarded as glorifying violence.

'Your father called me.'

'Why did my father call you?'

'He said you couldn't get in your flat. And that you think your mother's dead.'

I was feeling weak, so I nodded.

'I'll take care of it, OK, Mifti? Look at me.'

'Erm . . .'

'You go over to Charlene, she's waiting for you, she's made pasta with butter and sugar for the two of you.'

Instead of puking my guts out in her face, I caved in and set out on the five-minute trek to the sturdy block in which Charlene Kaplitz-Pittkowski and her family occupied a three-bedroom paradise with conservatory. I had to limp across a playground and then through a patch of

121

allotments. My leg hurt so much that I wished I could have chopped it off. When Charlene opened the door to me shyly in her blue and white striped tights, it seemed almost as if she was embarrassed at being four levels above me on the social scale from that day onward. She was one year older and sadly twenty years more retarded than me. In her room, we alternated between painting window pictures (ponies, Santa Claus, Shetland ponies) with special window picture paint and reading letters from fifteen-year-old girls to *Bravo* magazine about how a condom had got stuck somewhere in their cervix during sex.

Charlene: 'My mother just went so totally crazy when she found out you'd given me that Marilyn Manson CD, and then she confiscated it.'

'Did she say why?'

'She said it was crap and anyway it was a cover version and the cover version isn't as good as the version by the guy who sang it before.'

'That's true, actually.'

'Hey, hello? The guy who sang it before sang it like three hundred years ago, and that's so totally not cool.'

'No, Charlene, it's much cooler.'

'It's totally not cool, man.'

We were just listening to a cassette about two girls at a gymkhana when Charlene's mother knocked at the door. Obviously trying to prove something to me, she pointedly complimented Charlene on her pyjamas which she said looked really cool with turn-ups and all that. Then she said to me, 'Mifti, could you come outside for a minute?'

She didn't look at me again until I noticed there was an ambulance and two police cars outside our house. The downstairs door was open and I stomped up the stairs in a state of pseudo-calm, and our front door was open too, and just before I walked into the flat I was assailed by the stench of forty tons of puke and shit. Everything was covered in puke; wherever I looked some pool of puke triumphed at its victory over us.

The first thing I noticed was that my childhood drawings had been ripped off the walls, my elephant in the grass. Then I saw that our entire furnishings now consisted only of chunks of cherrywood scattered bleakly around the flat. You could no longer tell if they'd once been part of my shelves or my desk. The place I was standing in was made up solely of interblending shades of grey. In my mother's bedroom, six people in different coloured uniforms were attempting to put an end to her violent outbreak. She was biting and scratching and hitting out and screaming louder than I'd ever heard anyone scream. It was absolutely inhuman and repulsive. Blood was flowing from a hand – I wasn't sure whose it was. I stood in the doorway. She saw me before anyone else did, and fell silent. I ducked out of her sights.

She screamed, 'Mifti!'

Before I could leave the flat, she came stumbling out of her room and stopped motionless in front of me. She was wearing a royal blue polyester sweater and dirty knickers that had slipped down so far that every person in the flat was involuntarily confronted with her pubic hair. She was days away from starving herself to death. Her hair was stuck to her head and the corners of her mouth were bleeding. To my great dismay, all the strangers involved in the situation looked even worse than my mother, even though they were sober and clean, in contrast to her.

'Mifti,' she said again.

'Are you Mifti, madam? She's been calling for you the whole time.'

'Why are you calling me madam? I'm only ten.'

With these words, I ran down the stairs. Ms Kaplitz-Pittkowski croaked, 'Are you crying? Hey, Mifti, don't cry!'

She put her arms round me. I didn't resist because any rebellion would have given her too much insight into my mental state. I hated her. I hated my father for ringing her up.

'Does this happen often?'

'Of course not.'

The lasting reminders were a torn muscle in my left thigh and a ruptured ligament that ought to have been operated on. Two days later, my mother gave me my own key with a metal goldfish as a keyring. No comment was made. Nothing else happened.

3:20 a.m. Cold spreads across my skin; it can't be natural, it must be the result of some kind of cosmic rays caused by the Big Bang or something. My body falls asleep, trembling. I'm standing in a maisonette apartment straight out of an English blockbuster movie, grabbing a bald-headed man between the legs. By dint of writing the words 'sperm cunt' on the wall in lipstick, he proves he has an organic brain syndrome. Every pair of shoes I've ever owned is lined up according to size in the middle of the room. Spray-can cream and cake mixture spills out of them. A paranoia attack prompts me to leave the flat. Outside is nothing whatsoever. The entire world consists of construction rubble. When I go back inside, the flat has mutated into a hotel of above-average standard. The man and I walk up a stone spiral staircase, side by side. I know I've slept with him, but I can't get my head around when it must have been.

'Have you got any diseases or anything?'

'Why?'

'Because I want to know if I have to start worrying now.'

Through a swing door, we enter a wide corridor in which barred cages take the place of chandeliers. A selection of the most famous people in the world scream at us from the cages, in a language I've never heard before. Madonna is there and Marlon Brando and unfortunately that other weird guy, I can't remember his name right now, the one who always runs around like he's in the mafia. Now it's Ophelia walking by my side, wearing red overalls and not answering.

'What's up? Why aren't you answering? Are we going to carry on fucking at some point?'

'No.'

'Why not?'

'I don't fuck any more.'

'Jesus, man, I'm feeling so horny, though!'

'I'm not going to fuck you any more.'

'But why not?'

'I don't want to.'

'Are you positive?'

'Yes.'

'Pardon?'

'Yes.'

'Are you positive?'

'Yes. But you know I am.'

Everything's black and white because I can't see any colours any more.

I go and dance. Bryan Ferry tells me, 'We all spent Christmas in the totally classic way, really, as classic as you can get, it was UNBELIEVABLY classic. Until the fashionista faggot's little sister had the radical idea of holding some ritual on her deceased grandmother's property. We wrote down our wishes on slips of paper and ripped them to tiny pieces and scattered them on the wind and we wrote everything we wanted to leave behind on slips of paper too and then we threw them on the fire, though, well, you know. And last of all we all let out a huge primal scream.'

'Ah, the fashionista faggot, I see.'

He ceremoniously presents me with two tickets to Los Angeles, wrapped in paper printed with cartoon mice. 'You're in the wrong town, you should be in Hollywood!'

'Why are you giving me these?'

'Because it's your birthday.'

I look out of the window. It can't be true; today's not the 16th of August. There's snow on the ground. Within a matter of moments, I'm utterly convinced that I'm dreaming. If this is a dream, I think, the whole of humankind is doomed. I turn around, I bite my lips, I feel the wind, I realize it's all real, it's all three-dimensional.

'What can you do to wake up from one of these tricky in-between worlds, Bryan?'

As he doesn't answer and I want to try to make the best out of my inescapable situation, I throw myself out of the third-floor window. I fly for days over a landscape of glaciers.

Frustrated Women (I mean, they're frustrated)
(The Standells)

The ideal state of mind is just sailing through all the crap, high on adrenalin, thinking, what I'd really like to do now is play the lead role in a video for Donna Summer's 'I Feel Love', and anyway, woah, everything's gone pear-shaped, look, the sun's coming up. Our flat is flooded with rays of light squeezing in between the slats of the blinds. An unacceptable stench assails me. Edmond just happens to be one of those people whose favourite hobbies include nibbling at a honeydew melon someone else has already digested. Standing in his doorway, I watch in horror as my completely unclothed brother lies on his back snoring while someone else takes his photo. A man under the age of twenty-five who I've definitely never seen before is kneeling on the mint-green sheets with a digital SLR camera, zooming in on Edmond's dick. He's blond, wearing four-way stretch high-waist side zipper pants over black polyester shorts, and he gets the shock of his life when I give a rather over-ambitious cough just out of curiosity to see his face.

On his bare chest is an ornately lettered, *Earth provides enough to satisfy every man's need, but not every man's greed.*

Apart from that, there's absolutely nothing about him that might prompt spontaneous nausea right here and now, as über-attractive as he is, squatting there with his grey eyes and his guilty look, and his life's motto tattooed on his forehead: *My drugs phase will definitely be over tomorrow.*

'Holy shit, man! Which one of his sisters are you?'

'Mifti.'

Meanwhile, Edmond has plumped over on to his stomach and I can't stop staring at his poorly shaved sphincter.

'Haven't we been introduced at one of those concept-free parties with the "I wanna fuck" badges, Mifti?'

'Erm . . .'

'Never mind, I can't remember your face either. I really hate it anyway when all those idiots claim non-stop that they always remember faces but not names – I mean, how uncool is that? I personally much prefer remembering names than faces. And I'm perfectly open about it. So, Little Miss Butter Wouldn't Melt.'

'What?'

'I didn't even know Edmond was gay, by the way.'

'He isn't, if you ask me.'

'Why are you saying a thing like that? You're obviously not all that into anal sex?'

And then a sudden spontaneous wit emerges within me, taking me completely by surprise: 'No. Because I don't understand what's going on there. If they're good-looking I like just watching all those anally fixated women and men and thinking, great the way these beasts are moving and have a view of each other that catapults everything else into the background. Fantastic! I can certainly get a kick out of something I neither command nor enjoy. But I'm just not capable of getting any deeper into the material or making a more complicated judgement of what you do and how good it is. Still, it's impressive, that whole act of violence.'

'Yeah!'

'What's your name anyway?'

'Just call me Smoothio.'

Edmond croaks: 'Water, water!' and waves his arms impassively to draw attention to himself. Smoothio and I try to trickle flat Diet Coke into his mouth, breaking out in several fits of hysterical laughter. Meanwhile, the shaved sphincter turns out to be the most difficult aspect to digest, what with my sibling's only warning to repeatedly permeate the whole anti-authoritarian up-bringing in a big-brotherly tone consisting of the advice, 'Mifti, if you shave your sphincter you're shaving your whole life away!'

My life, his bedroom, his Ferrari T-shirt, his shaved sphincter and our top-banana genes.

Right now it's all about the deconstruction of daylight anyway, or a new definition of moral values, and apart from that it's about a decaff cinnamon cappuccino with amaretto and about the fact that we've run out of cigarettes and about the ineluctable continuation of alcohol consumption. It's quarter past eight and the sun's screaming at me in anything but a subtle manner, telling me I should have closed the curtains long ago. It's one of those moments right now when not even more vodka or any of these parallel-world add-ons to my consciousness are capable of digging out a channel within me that's willing to survive. Everything that happens takes three seconds.

If I get up off this nut-wood-look stackable chair right now, I'll manage two stumbling steps towards the bathroom and then collapse.

ALICE KNOWS IT, I KNOW IT, GOD KNOWS IT.

'So you suspect your brother isn't even gay?'

'He's as bi as they come. So there's no need for you to feel offended in any way if he suddenly stumbles out of here, says his goodbyes and swings off on his bike to the Thai brothel on Kopenhagener Strasse. And then he'll tell some petite black-haired beauty with fantastic olive-skinned legs how much it turns him on that her skin looks the same all over, even her armpits, and two seconds later she'll find herself underneath him getting a seriously substandard shag through her fishnets. That's just what he's like, huh? Why – d'you like him then?'

'He looks like David Hasselhoff, for fuck's sake! I'll put on a motorbike helmet and break his face if he wants to fuck around with dumb Thai cunts. Are you as bi as they come as well?'

'I hardly jumped for joy when I found out about it, but yeah, I'm as bi as they come as well.'

'Hot shit.'

Then minutes of meaty silence. I just can't deal with this right now, I just can't manage to take a toke on the joint held in my direction for some time. My hand keeps missing it.

At some point Smoothio's suddenly like, 'Fuck, what was that noise?'

'Huh?'

'There was just this really weird noise thingy just now.'

'That was the joint in my big toe cracking.'

'No, it was – Jesus, I dunno, what was it? What direction did it even come from?'

'Oh shit!'

Someone is interfering with our front door, certain of victory over it.

'I urgently have to barricade myself into some kind of bullet-proof larder!' I say, pretty determined, and Smoothio responds simply.

'Holy shit, Mifti, you just got up and fell right over! I just closed my eyes for a moment for various reasons and then I open them up again and you're not upright any more, you're like lying around, and now you're still lying there. Crazy, I've never seen anything like it, I swear! You just fell right over!'

Everything's spinning, the shards of crockery next to me are spinning, a couple of months ago a coffee machine exploded here and the resulting stains on the ceiling are not only spinning, they're suddenly evolving into combatant baby animals on bikes with five-cylinder rotating engines. Annika starts spinning too when she comes shuffling into the kitchen with her back bent over. It takes her ten minutes to take her jacket off, and as she does so she explains to us three times over in various different tones of voice that she ought to have been at the agency five minutes ago, in theory.

'We're just talking about bisexuality!' I segue elegantly over to her.

'Um, I'm hetero!' she says with her eyes closed, and Smoothio regurgitates a semi-digested portion of blue-berry yogurt into our polka-dot teapot. Monday morning – perfect, in an hour at most our housekeeper will be standing outside the front door announcing with great fervour that she'd have baked us a cake if her husband hadn't died of a stroke last night.

I don't dare to think about tomorrow, in fact I don't even dare to think at all.

I turn my music up too loud, I dance too much, I go over the top in everything I do just so I don't attract my own attention any more. I wait. Wait to fall asleep, to go crazy, to get up again and go in the kitchen, to turn myself into a Colombian black-spined toad on the kitchen windowsill. OK, and my answer to every question anyone asks me is, 'Everything's great, I'm just trying to decide on the basis of all my thoughts and fantasies and impulses and actions revolving around my own death how long it'll take until I bleed to death at last.'

Then at some point I head round to Simon's place in Neukölln, because he's just always stoned and has a two-thousand-euro Siamese cat and about forty aquariums full of these little amphibian-type creatures for sale. I gaze at a nocturnal Mexican salamander, shocking pink or at least very, very pink indeed. It has funny little tentacles, beady blue eyes and the friendliest smile I've ever seen. Crazy shit.

'That's a baby axolotl,' says Simon.

'An axolotl?'

'A baby axolotl. It has the friendliest smile on the whole planet – take it with you. It looks like a comic character, it's really low-maintenance and it reaches sexual maturity without ever undergoing metamorphosis out of the amphibian stage – it just never grows up. Crazy, huh?'

'Can it turn in a circle?'

'What?'

I really do go right ahead and buy the dumb axolotl off him, carrying it around with me for ages in a see-through plastic bag filled with water.

My lung says its farewells and I keep on running, my heart skips a beat and I keep on running, the mucous membranes start coming out of my nostrils, having painfully separated from the mechanically delineated organ surfaces, and I run past a long-haired passer-by in a Hawaiian shirt, who stutters wildly into a microphone pointed in his direction: 'I think flirting's generally very good, and, er, it depends on the, er, how you flirt, what you – I mean not like dodgy chat-up lines, I mean more laid-back, not all that macho stuff, more like you have a nice conversation and then you end up picking someone up. I'm lucky, you know, I go to the kind of establishments where you find classy women, let's say, and then you get talking and it always works, I always end up in bed with someone, let's say. And if you ask me, it's great, you just mustn't start in with the funny jargon in that whole naff way. You have to reach women via their feelings, so I tell them, hey, nice outfit, and that works every time. You take that feelings route and you get everything you want. That's how I'd interpret it.'

As the sun goes down, it starts to rain like that whole meat-coloured early summer shit, and I stomp across town with my eyes down. Circular arcs of light reflect from scattered puddles. Outside the door to Ophelia's apartment, I try to suppress the nausea rising inside me at the thought of her irregular features. I knock. A guy of over-average height with greasy hair opens up. He looks at me like an aggressive bulldog and yells, not taking his eyes off me, 'Have you got a new girlfriend, Ophelia?'

From what feels like two miles away, Ophelia shrieks back, 'Shut up, man, I love her and I'm gonna look after her, she's the first goddamn person in my whole life I'm gonna look after voluntarily!'

She comes running to the door in two-inch high mules,

staring at me out of breath, with her mouth open and mascara dried hard on her red-stained face. As she drags me into the flat, she leads me to understand, with all the egocentric nervousness that makes up her existence, how crap everyone else is and that I'm the only person whose face she doesn't want to puke in.

The bulldog says, 'So the result is that I'll have to look after both of you from now on.'

'So what if you do?'

'Who is this guy?'

'Foxy.'

'Foxy comes across as if the main purpose of his life is phlegming up on carpets. Is he living here right now?'

'Foxy's a literature lecturer.'

A mega-bony girl with black-lined eyes is sitting in the kitchen.

'Are you living here right now?'

'Yeah, because – I dunno.'

I take a bottle of whisky out of the kitchen cupboard and sit down on Ophelia's lap, seeing as the fourth kitchen chair appears to be missing. There's a smell of hash, baked trout and sweat. Last night Ophelia was informed over the telephone that her father had died of bowel cancer. She shows me a couple of photos she's taken of herself on her digital SLR camera. A woman absolutely shattered and broken leaps out at me from the tiny screen, blessed with the omnipotence to plunge anyone confronted by these photos into a state of impotence. Although we're veering between diarrhoea, dizziness and mortal fear, the four of us are kicking it with an attitude of absolute elegance. Foxy the bulldog asks if I'm OK; apparently I look really upset, as if I felt both dehydrated and superfluous at the same time.

'You've been taking drugs, haven't you?!' he says.

I don't answer, of course.

'And how old are you?'

Ophelia: 'Stop it, will you? Mifti can look after herself much better than all of us put together.'

And I go, 'Sixteen.'

'Sixteen? She's sixteen? And you're trying to tell me she can look after herself in some way?'

'Do you seriously want to have a conversation about my drug problem?'

'D'you even know what we're talking about here?'

'What then?'

'Jesus Christ, you're sixteen years old and you're sitting here in the kitchen of a barely functioning twenty-eight-year-old woman and you look like you've been trying to come down from a seven-week trip for the past three days. It's absolute self-destruction, in five years' time you'll either be dead or, in the best case, you'll be working cash-in-hand in a suburban travel agency.'

Dark-haired fungal-infested skank (mortally offended): 'Hey, hey, hey, hey!'

Foxy: 'Hey, come on, it's true!'

The dark-haired fungal-infested skank blows her nose – it's all too much for her.

Foxy: 'Look at Alessa, Mifti, look her right in the eye. She works on the side in a travel agency because her benefits aren't nearly enough to cover all her excessive needs. Heroin's like a child, your whole life revolves around it and suddenly you wake up stinking in a shit-filled bathtub – that's your official bed and you're not even capable of questioning your state, let alone doing anything to change it. Picking up a heroin habit is comparable to having children, I'm not kidding.'

I'm like, 'I'm not going to pick up a heroin habit, it's just that I keep thinking, shit, my legs are ten feet long and so elastic!'

'And what exactly else is going on? In your head, I mean?'

'Oh, no idea, really. What d'you want to hear? Everything's kind of fluffy, mystical, my skin's fucked, everything inside me's going soft, I stink to high heaven, I haven't had a shower for three days and, oh shit, the floor's three-dimensional! D'you want to know what I'm thinking about while I chuck all this in your face like the slimy corpse of a squirrel? A few months ago I was standing in the kitchen next to my father, whose mind was occupied with some crap or other, and I had an orange and a knife, and I asked him, like, "Hey, Dad, I don't know how to peel an orange without it getting really annoying." He didn't react so I carried on annoying him really badly, I mean I really had this serious problem and I had to get it solved. "Please, Dad!" And he yelled, "Mifti, all you have to do is simply cut it into segments like a pumpkin, there's really no reason to explain to a fifteen-year-old semi-adult how to peel a bloody orange!" And there was nothing I could do but carve a smiley face into the orange. If it hadn't gone mouldy it'd still be there now.'

'Top story.'

'D'you want to hear another joke?'

'You're really wasted, Mifti.'

'Three days after the whole orange shit my father wanted to take me out cruising down Friedrichstrasse in his BMW to show me the house I was born in. By the way, I didn't even know I was born in Berlin until that moment, I got the shock of my life. Anyway, so we got out of the car and trotted through to the backyard, and then there was this stupid little climbing frame, it was like an improvised playground installation, and we're like smack bang in front of this climbing frame made of old ropes and stuff. And my dad asks if I remember it. I say no, as you might expect. And he's suddenly like: "You really don't? When you were two you climbed up to the top like greased lightning and then you just fell down on purpose through the hole in the middle. Crazy, huh? You weren't messing about or anything, you were just firmly convinced you could fly. You were pretty confused when you landed on the sand, kid. That's when I first thought, this kid's crazy. Oh boy, this girl's really something special.'

'At that moment all I felt like doing was weeping bitterly, but I couldn't. I wanted to freeze that impulse to cry so I could thaw it out later and remember it and then scream and shout hysterically when nobody would notice. It was an incredibly liberating idea, but I really can't reproduce the whole crap any more. So anyway we got back in the car and listened to Verdi. Verdi's actually just pop, mood music with no credibility, the perfect accompaniment for thinking up mass murder strategies. And I realized two things at that moment. Firstly that Verdi, Wagner and I only despise each other because all our razzle-dazzle sensationalism is so similar. And secondly that all this is tantamount to nothing but deepest sadness. I could have been thinking about so many things, had so many really serious ideas. Like the question of what you see when you have an orgasm, a Gothic cathedral or baby animals. I dunno, all I ever see is cheddar cheese melted under neon lights and beer garden tables just about to collapse under my weight. I mean, that whole unbearable horniness that's somehow even based on mutual consent is the main reason for my excessive identification with Patti Smith – because on the evening of my twelfth birthday, when a completely naive impulse made me strut around the changing room in a state of greater undress and provocation than absolutely necessary, when the two of us were alone for the first time, when my admiration for him evolved into a desire for him mingled with deep, deep disgust, I felt like I was surrounded by horses. Horses, horses, horses, horses. Coming at me from all directions. Shiny white horses, their heads going up in flames. Punk. I could've been thinking about punk or the fact that I'd be pretty fucked if I didn't pass my exams. Or about Frau Simmrohs limping down the corridor still wondering why I held a talk about the common mallard instead of the assignment she set on photosynthesis. About how to gain basic knowledge of trigonometry of my own accord. Why my tights are laddered, why my skin's so scarily rough, why my father has had absolutely nothing against me chain-smoking in his car for some time now. About how everything goes on. Everything keeps going on. About my neighbour texting me the other day that he had an animal story for me about Paul the baby squirrel that fell asleep in the palm of his hand in White Trash with his tail in a vodka and tonic, and a couple of days later the two of them went to Lake Garda. I could at least have wondered why there's no guarantee that the sky won't suddenly fall in. But all that seemed so freaking petty in comparison to the realization that the apatosaurus igitur definitely didn't waste a thought on whether it might look ridiculous sixty-five million years ago. It didn't give a shit what kind of impression it made and that whole superficiality didn't even exist, back then, you know what I'm saying?'

I gasp for air, deeply upset that such a load of utter crap just came out of my mouth. Alessa asks me, 'Are you the mysterious gifted child then who got raped as well? Is that why you two are friends?'

I look at Ophelia, and Ophelia says, 'It was all completely different – I was six and I got fucked up the arse on holiday and I was such a poor little neglected rich kid that nobody believed me. I suspect the major problem is that you think you're a sexualized child and you can deal with it.'

'Did you just say you were a poor little neglected rich kid?'

'Yeah, Mifti. Just look at Foxy.'

Heroin, well, you know, it's kinda sorta uncool in the year 2009. As I look over at him, Foxy puts on a kind face to suggest that even I might as well go ahead and take it, at least to throttle my excessive party pulse-rate down from three hundred and twenty to a healthy ninety. I'm completely freaking out, and at the same I really don't give a shit what I take next, even though my diaphragm starts to distort unpleasantly in the wrong direction even at the thought of the words, 'I did my first line of heroin when I was sixteen and now I'm nineteen and I look like I'm thirty-eight.' I go over to Ophelia, who's starting to cry yet again, and bite her on the neck, and as I do so I realize I'm definitely too weak to stand up to the peer pressure building up here.

'Go away, honey!' sobs Ophelia.

'No.'

'Hey, sweetheart, let go of me and go and sit down again over there.'

I sit down in one corner, as far away from the heroin as possible. A remnant of intelligence prompts me to make that decision – not a bad thing. I was told my mother was dead in a mustard-yellow room, sitting all alone and abandoned on a hard chair, and suddenly this doctor, whose face I've sadly blanked out of my memory, gives me an absolutely unfamiliar approach to life. As he uttered the words that I'd be on my own from now on, my head moved to the left, forcing my eyes to stare out of the window into absolute blackness. The fact that her death added this level of blackness to my perception is too high a price for the words, 'My mother died when I was thirteen.'

But still, those words are actually all I have left now. I haven't got a dedicated parent or guardian and I haven't got a favourite leisure activity, I didn't even have a mother, all I've really got left is these words, no kidding.

'Do you want to take it or not?'

'I'm not quite sure.'

'You don't have to if you don't want to.'

The line cut specially for me is held out generously. I grab the saucepan lid out of Alessa's hand.

'OK, so you do want to,' she says, majorly annoyed. Me, the heroin, its addictive potential and a skin full of goosebumps run out of the kitchen and down the hall to Ophelia's bedroom, and my answer to the question posed in a droning singsong by three different mouths – 'Hey, what's up with you? Where are you going?' – is, 'I get the feeling I have to make some kind of ceremony out of this, guys, that means on my own and on a comfortable visco-elastic mattress, and I may also provide a soundtrack of appropriate music for the event!'

'Speaking of music, the other night I dreamed me and Emre made a whole load of little Turkish baby boys, and one of them scratched my "Blue Monday" record.'

'"Blue Monday"? You keep celebrating some rebirth of New Order that never even took place, it's disgusting. They're out. They're just plain old out.'

And suddenly they fall silent, the drugs putting everything out of action once and for all. I don't use the light switch, nor do I think of simply tipping the line out of the window. There's a pleasant twilight atmosphere going on outside. I sit cross-legged on the bed and reach for a post-it note to roll up, with two Austrian phone numbers and the name 'Will o' the Wisp' written on it. OK. Now we have it. I vacuum up the craving for absolute intensity in life. I close my eyes as a reflex. In slow motion, I see tiny crystals rushing up my mucous membranes, battling their way into my bloodstream and then exploding there within a fraction of a second, to an extent that whips me against the headboard. I tear my eyes open and try to grab hold of the last tiny spark of realistic ugliness, but some primal force out-trumps me, not putting my perception or my muscle contraction impulse out of action, but only that centuries-old consensus among all the do-gooders in this world, according to which every living individual tries to battle their way to some surface or other from the cradle to the grave. The bed tips to the left. I slide slowly towards the floorboards, dragging the sheet off the mattress. Heroin is not one of those approaches to human life that offers diffuse promises, it's the only way to decode the word 'life' as what it is: nothing whatsoever. The zone of sacred law violation. Heroin is the surface. I'm gonna tell you exactly what I'm feeling, because you never say

anything: I'm feeling absolutely nothing. Nothing whatsoever. If there's anything, anything other than your
love, which can and will lead me back to the arrogance
with which I embarked on this journey through all this
messed-up shit, then it's probably the apathy I now
know.

Dear Alice,
    I feel the need to communicate with you but find
it absolutely impossible, because I'm scared. Scared
as if to death of saying these words, of saying any
words. You don't need to doubt this fearing, my
fear has many reasons.
    If fear wasn't necessary, we by now would have
found ourselves travelling down a road. How can I
be telling you that I need you and simultaneously
believe equally, that is, totally, another reality that
lacerates? I'd love to look like you, so that every
time you stare at me and yet still don't say anything,
you see every pulsing pus of eczema, every tiny piece
of rotting flesh, every skin crater, every boil, every
malignant cancerous carcinoma. May you only have
fallen in love with me for the sole purpose of being
confronted every moment with every characteristic
you despise: with yourself. M.

All I think any more is: that's why. That's why I'm not
regarded as socially acceptable by generally accepted
standards, and that's why I don't have my sights on the
target of being utterly suitable for some kind of normal
labour market – because it's just not about whether you
experience something or miss out on it, all it's about is
the degree of intensity, isn't it, Madonna? A moment like

that can't be planned. Are you hanging out in the next-door flat right now, with a waxwork of the Pope and forty puppy dogs flown in specially?

'Sorry, but fuck! The Liars are the fucking most awesomely fucking wicked band on the whole bastard planet! Aaaah! I'm completely flipping out, I have to shag a huge freaking cliff!'

'I'm just that "He only told his own girlfriend about the three hundred male sexual partners on holiday in Tanzania when his AIDS test was positive and he had to secretly escape to South America" kinda guy. I just have a couple of bad habits.' 'I don't know who you guys are and why you shot at him, but if you want to stay here you're gonna have to stop shooting at each other.' 'You can sell someone a baby polar bear as a dog, you know.' 'Right now I'm Bianca Jagger, Snoopy's biggest titty groupie.'

I REMEMBER EVERYTHING, what the hell's going on here, what is this? Jesus.

'Hey, Mifti, Alessa used to study medicine and she did a spell on the psychiatry ward as well, as you do, and I don't know if I should tell you this but do you know what kind of prognosis you had?' 'Huh?' 'Do you want to tell her, Alessa?' 'What d'you mean, prognosis?' 'Well, you know, in your situation and state of mind, whatever.' 'So?' 'Purely palliative, you get me? You were something like an incurable case for the psychiatry ward.' 'What, you mean – oh. That's why they were all so "I don't care"? You mean they'd just given up on me? They didn't think I was dumb or anything, they just thought ... FUCK!' 'Statistically, your chances were

144

close to zero. In all probability they still are. Mine too. Let me take you by the hand, and I know why Alessa told me and why I'm telling you now, for fuck's sake, WE GOT THE GODDAMN POTENTIAL TO RULE EVERYTHING! I've got a little admission to make, sweetheart: I'm not twenty-eight, I'm thirty-six. As you can imagine, I can't cope with life the way I ought to at my age. I've never told you that because I was so scared it would relativize everything or change things in some way. Scared you'd look at me differently. Or that my photos aren't what they ought to be, as soon as I'm in my oddball inexorably ageing freaking position and it's no longer OK to have no idea how everything works, you know, love and life and stuff. I keep asking myself: how could this happen? Why am I still incapable of anything but permanent coquettishness with my state of unconsciousness, this constant anti-capitalism that always operates on a moral basis and considers itself morally integer; anti-capitalism as a self-preservation instinct, so to speak? I exploit resentments, like against bankers for example, to defend myself against the superfluity of my own existence. Why do I wake up one morning with a ten year stretch in my life when nothing worth mentioning has changed, except for my bank balance? That's the question my drug-abused physical constitution has started asking me three times a day – it's now totally detached from my mind. It didn't used to be that way; we used to be a team, my body, my mind, my promising future and me. I feel like I've had amnesia for years. My brain just stood still from nineteen ninety-nine to two thousand and eight, and now everything's out of sync. I'm four million levels below you guys in the food chain and I hate myself and everyone else. I just had to get that out.' 'My father thinks I've messed him up and my own life too. Maybe he's right. I lied too much, I caused too much mistrust, and now at the end of the day I'm totally paranoid because of course I feel like I can't change anything any more, apart from using long words in the wrong context and everyone leaving me and rocking on through all the crap like a complete bitch from hell. Nobody ever taught me to deal with conflicts. Someone recommended I try building an anger den to get it out of my system. Has he gone to sleep over there?' 'Who is Alice anyway?' 'Whoa, how nice and simple for your father! And if it wasn't you, who would have messed up his life? Your mother? Your sister? His hundred and ninety-three lovers? The housekeeper? The postman?' 'There's really nothing going on here right now.' 'At first I wanted to laugh, but then – pah!' 'The moment is sooo gone.' 'I've just been your intern for the past twenty seconds.' 'Then go and get me the waffle maker and minced pork right now.' 'And the fifty-stone corpse for dipping.' 'I'll bring you the bicycle pump as well.' 'OK.' 'My father's wife, on the other hand, has recently been widowed, as you know. We talked on the phone today.' 'Yeah, we know that.' 'And she told me in this tear-choked voice how they resuscitated him three times in a row. The first time round, like once he'd been clinically dead for the first time and then alive for five minutes in between, she said he demanded more re-animation. No way did he want to die for good, no way.' 'Crash course in depressing music, part one.' 'Explain the general truth in one sentence: Wu-Tang Clan ain't nothing to fuck with. Kim Gordon is the woman of the millennium. My Bloody Valentine, a hundred and forty dB, oops, I've just gone deaf. The MDMA man, is no horse.' 'Crash course in depressing music, part two. Robert Wyatt, "At Last I Am Free".' 'To be perfectly honest, all I can do right now is laugh like an idiot.' 'Tell the rest of that animal story about the crazy squirrel in the vodka and tonic.' 'It even started off mega-absurd. You have to imagine Lars as a slightly degenerate guy with a long red fringe and white dandruff on his black sweatshirt jacket, standing under the ultra-violet lighting in that bunker club. And along comes this really nice girl. She says, "Hey, I'll give you twenty euros if you look after my baby squirrel while I go to the toilet." And Lars really adores animals more than anything else, especially squirrels, so he says, "Jesus, I'll give you twenty euros if you LET ME look after your squirrel."' 'Does anyone fancy crazy non-stop-talking comedy characters? I just got a text from someone called Stefan asking me if I'm going to THE WEDDING today. A pond scum of digested anti-capitalist material forming on top of a group of crazy comedy characters. What motherfucking wedding does he mean? I hate texts like this. And what scum is he talking about?' 'Oh shit.' 'What?' 'The wedding.' 'Wait, tell me which Stefan might be in possession of my mobile number?' 'Isn't he that nonsense farce guy whose villa we went to and the sprinkler system turned on for some inexplicable reason, and later he leaned out of the car on the way to Schlachtensee and said, "Excuse the testosterone, we've gone all evening without testosterone and now it's just breaking out of me, sorry"?!' 'Yeah, it could be him.' 'Albrecht and Samantha, wedding, Richard-Wagner-Strasse. I completely forgot about it, guys.' 'Isn't Emre DJing there?' 'I think I'm gonna puke.' 'Shall I call us a cab?' 'Yeah. Oh fuck, you know, the fur-coated sixth-former and the restaurateur and Emre and – the thing with Emre is a thing about music and nothing else. So about everything in the world. And nothing. It's nothing to do with heterosexuality.' 'Why is laughing like an idiot all you can do, Mifti?' 'It's a thing about AIDS too, don't forget.' 'I just can't contribute anything to this situation except idiotic laughter. I know there'll never be anything more awesome in my life than heroin. From now on I'll compare everything that happens with this morbid upper middle-class heroin trip that's just taking off. I don't even get that you're all here, I so don't give a shit about you. Not one single moment in my entire life will ever match up to the perfection going down right now. How long's it going to last?' 'I'd guess seventy minutes, tops.' 'So the best time in my life will be over in seventy minutes?' 'Tops.' 'We can trust the MDMA man. He's his own best customer. He's no horse.' 'Has anyone got an alternative taxi number? This one's permanently engaged!' 'Woah, crazy, I thought you said before that MDMA's no horse!' 'The MDMA man's no horse.' 'Oh well, OK. Seventy minutes.'

8:40 p.m. Once Ophelia has slammed the front door behind her and realized her key's not in her handbag but on the kitchen floor, we treat ourselves to a spot of socializing terror before the world comes to an end. The two-hundred-year-old neighbour's doorbell is rung, and instead of greeting us with the words, 'Hello, I'm two hundred years old and you wouldn't believe all I've seen,' she's in her in underwear, a big fat plaster over her right eye. There follows a great deal of reciprocal cursing, some kind of coat hanger is handed over, which is to be bent into shape at 7 a.m. tomorrow so that it fits into the lock, reciprocal backs are patted for normality achieved in an emergency, and now at last the illegible words are written on the huge dance floor as it slams the shit at a hundred and forty dB: *On thy house too may I bring the curse*. Instead of finding an alternative taxi number, we decide in mutually overflowing inspiration to hire a car, because that's kinda cool anyway. Foxy knows someone in Lichtenberg, so we stroll on out to Lichtenberg, totally mentally disturbed, taking ages to reach a mouldering car-hire place in the dark grey of the rising night. A milky veil has settled over the path we've trodden. A guy with fat teeth and irregular facial hair heads for Foxy with his arms akimbo and says, 'Oh man, last time I saw you, you had fake dreads and now you've suddenly got a black crop cut, would you look at you!'

The two of them take turns grouching at each other, five yards away from us next to a BMW 1 Series convertible. Four minutes later the guy comes over to us with the keys to the BMW. Seeing as I'm only capable of doing as I'm told right now, I watch myself entering my PIN number on the card reader held out to me. For some inexplicable reason a hundred and sixty euro is debited from my account. Before I end up cowering on the back seat next to Ophelia, trying to watch Foxy starting the engine and whatsit-ing the roof back at the same time, we all take a seat together on a kerb behind various small VWs and get through what feels like three kilos of coke. I notice it's now no longer about the effect, it's just a kind of nasal gratification, and at the same time I remember the idea Ophelia had a couple of weeks ago, of always combating suicide attempts with a cocaine overdose. She was of the opinion that before you've consumed enough to seriously kill yourself, your personal world view ought to have changed so much for the positive that you really don't fancy being digested and shat out again by dumb maggots under the earth three days later. I said, 'Can I join your club?'

And she's like, 'Yeah.'

So that's that.

The wedding is in a 4,000-square-foot apartment in West Berlin. We've struggled up six flights of stairs and are heavy-breathing outside a slightly open door, through which an acceptable bassline boxes its way out – out of this unbearably laid-back semi-private party shit.

Looking down at myself, I realize I've been wearing a jumper decorated with an appliqué squirrel for about four days. And for more than six hours, I summon up briefly while I'm at it, my right hand has been gripping this plastic bag filled with fresh water and the axolotl.

'Great wedding present,' someone says.

And I answer, 'I'm not a criminal, I'm just not looking all that good right now.'

The axolotl's stopped smiling. The flat is spilling over with people sipping their drinks, swathed in asymmetry, hysteria and satin – in other words, everything that makes a good party dress – and some of the guests have smeared some kind of glitter stuff on their faces. The surroundings are slightly too wood-panelled for my taste. I stand in the doorway of a bathroom remodelled into a highly frequented chill-out area and watch Hersilie, who played 'Killing Me Softly' on a grand piano we came across in the lobby of the Maritim Grand Hotel the other week, after two Bacardis at twelve euros a pop. Right now she's sitting on the edge of a bathtub and disqualifying herself in the eyes of several bored-looking men by narrating a sex disaster related to her preference for knitwear, gesticulating wildly. I'm listening with equal measures of horror and amusement, when suddenly her fatally distraught boyfriend Georg drags me away from the doorway. Why's this arsehole wearing a fur coat and two pairs of sunglasses?

He says, 'Shit, can you please do something about this?'

'I don't feel responsible for anything whatsoever today, Georg. I've just come as a discursive extra, me and my axolotl.'

'Mifti, those two guys are supposed to be financing my next project about the everyday objects sealed in plastic document pockets, and apart from that they're a totally humour-free zone. If they're reminded at the office tomorrow morning that Hersilie's here with me, they'll think I'm absolutely out of the question.'

'Hersilie's your girlfriend, sweetheart!'

'And what do you think I should do now, for God's sake?'

'Nothing at all. Just be glad she always brings along her own party tent, unlike the humour-free zone over there.'

'But can't she ever take the party tent off, at least today?'

'To be honest I don't think it comes off any more.'

'Oh God.'

'What would you prefer, Georg? Collective anal retentiveness or . . .'

A strained-looking man in polyester shorts pushes between us and wants to join in the discussion. As far as I'm aware I've never seen the guy before in my life.

'Collective anal retentiveness? How does that come about then?'

Georg looks the guy up and down and says, 'Er, Mifti, have you two met? This is, er . . .'

'Yes, I think we know each other, you're . . . shit, hang on, I know for sure we've met before, um . . .'

'I'm Smoothio, we were introduced at that party where you only got in with a badge saying, "I wanna fuck." I slept with your brother yesterday.'

'Mmmh.'

And Georg says, just before he realizes he's messed up the situation and has to disappear a.s.a.p.: 'Oh, kiddo, don't worry about it, I can't remember him either.'

I look at Smoothio. He's looking really shit by now.

'I was actually there when you were sleeping with my brother.'

'Oh yeah, true, sorry.' He hugs me and gurgles some disconnected crap. I'm just about to turn my back on him with no further comment when he adds to his stammering, suddenly perfectly clear, 'There's definitely something fishy going on when someone sweats right through two jumpers like you.'

'Huh?'

'Your body seems to be secreting some pretty nasty stuff right now. Pretty hardcore – just now you sweated right through your jumper and mine too!'

'Oh man.'

'Yup.'

'See you later.'

I'm not interested in the over-dimensioned neutrality of the situation, I'm not interested in the wolf's-headed glitter ball stuck half-heartedly to the ceiling, and I'm not interested in the beat driving up my pulse from all directions, even though my blood pressure is about to explode some blood vessel responsible for supplying my lung tissue. I spot Jürgen in the distance, his cry of joy thirty per cent down to my presence and seventy per cent down to some in-law of a big-time entrepreneur being drafted in to wander around putting up to three grams of coke in selected guests' back pockets. There's ecstasy punch as well. All I want is water. A plastic cup of water to wash this bastard shortness of breath away and let me be something other than this embodiment of mega-claustrophobic FEAR getting bashed by one elbow protruding from a T-shirt sleeve after the next. Cheering, transparent plastic chairs, candlelight, a man with close-set eyes, whose shoulder I've just accidentally rested my chin on. I'm starting to feel how incredibly good he looks in his motto sweatshirt, presumably printed with fluffy lettering by some up-and-coming designer. He stands perfectly still, holding my right hand, until I relax and he comes closer and says, 'You're allowed to breathe, by the way.'

'I kind of can't breathe any more.'

My hand on the back of his neck, alternating between lying flat on his shoulder and clenching like a fist. His stomach and thighs against my stomach, my thighs. My lips, terribly, close to his ear. The slightest change in the pressure of his hand on my back alters our motion. In an attempt to maintain my tenderness by any conceivable means, I unfortunately say the terrible words, 'Touch me.'

He puts his hand on my head with slightly too much emphasis, and I tremble, because of the things rising up inside of me, because of this awful situation and my lust for life – what can I do, all he has to do is reach out his hand for me again. I look on at the whole scene without the slightest reaction, his fingers try to de-torque my greasy hair, all the horror vanishing down the plughole, and as soon as a tiny trace of desire's involved, I freeze like a little bastard of a know-it-all struck by lightning. When he kisses me it means war. I look at a thread of saliva I've left behind between jet-black stubble on his cheek, and turn around.

He throws me a nagging, 'What's that stupid creature you're lugging round with you the whole time?'

In the meantime, Samantha's taxi-driving father has got himself tattooed as well as the happy couple. How delightful. He can now parade around Neukölln with the face of David Hasselhoff engraved into his lower arm. *I cum in my sister's body lotion.*

In the furthest corner of my eye, Ophelia is just adopting a position enabling her to see what record Emre's putting on next. *I love it when the little slut rubs my sperm all over her skin.*

It's not just conflicting feelings he's landed her with, it's the biggest and baddest crap in her whole life. Because she used to love him. He was the first person she really seriously loved, that arsehole. And normally he spends all day yelling, 'GOOD LIFE', in a sun-soaked London apartment. They both had this sick passion for Brian Wilson, because he's so sick and all that, *Pet Sounds* is just so dark dark dark. Last autumn I listened to Ophelia laying down the whole complicated relationship issue under a Japanese flowering cherry tree outside her front door. 'I love the world, I love baby foals, I love adjectives just like you, I love Görlitzer Park, I love women. And men are just kind of dumb,' she said. 'I

154

wrote a whole novel when I was twelve, patched together entirely out of Nick Cave lyrics. "Next to me lies the print of your body plan like the map of a forbidden land."'

Bryan Ferry: 'Where would you go if you were me?'

Unsuccessful faces distorted by hate wherever you look.

'What, running, huh?' 'D'you still go jogging on the track next to the Mauerpark?' 'No, I only do yoga now.' 'I'm not quite sure whether I ought to find the girl over there interesting or sad.' 'But when you do yoga they like fix you with your back to the wall and then you have to do the, shit, what's it called, doggy position? Joey, is it called doggy position, do you know about yoga and stuff?' 'That's the mega-underage sister of that marketing bitch and the cool words jungle brother.' 'Poor little precocious girl.' 'Dog, that's it.'

'But it's interesting to see what happens when you give a stage to some deadly boring teenage drama.'

'Anyway, in the dog when you do yoga you have to bend over these funny piled-up blocks, and after that my back always hurts like hell.'

'I always find it so crazy the way people take her so seriously. Why does a sixteen-year-old young thing who's constantly slipping into hardcore arrogance and using empty phrases get invited to a party like this? Is she still at school?'

'What blocks?' 'She's a drug addict, how's she supposed to go to school?' 'I bet she puts her hand up in German class and asks if she can pop over to the chemistry lab to get her heroin fixed up over a Bunsen burner.' 'Blocks?' 'She really gets on my tits. Acts like she's skipped puberty and now she's fighting against having to catch up on it. She can't listen properly either, all those empty phrases and the constant "Yeah, yeahs" to every question you ask her – how hard is that to deal with, huh?' 'What blocks is he talking about?' 'I know this girl about the same age and she talks the same, completely strenuous, people tend to overvalue that kind of person, in my humble opinion.' 'You know, blocks. There's not that many different kinds of blocks, are there?' 'You're right, by the way, I think. Precociousness plays a big, big role in the whole thing.'

I'm a bad person. I'm a sick person. But mainly I'm the only person for miles around who can claim in all seriousness to be absolutely unscrupulous, despite the anti-megalomania stance put on hold for years and the constant shouts of, 'At the end of the day everything takes place according to the fundamental laws of increased consciousness and the inactivity resulting from those laws, with the consequence that everything is relative "and nothing can be changed and if we do have to live then at least do it in a nice French chateau" life principles rubbish.' What's behind this unscrupulousness? Is it my extensive experience of life? The iron-shaped scar on my back? Is it because I was taught to respond to the comment, 'I bet you'd rather be hugged than hug someone else,' with the words, 'Yeah, from the day I was born'? Is it my shattered knee joints? My sensitivity to temperature, the cigarettes extinguished on my skin, some genetic defect, burnt-out synapses and all this anger at having to wake up every morning in a general state of fear?

I have no trouble watching a fully conscious six-year-old getting her retinas burnt out with boiling sulphur while some dick gets rammed up her arse simultaneously, and after that she bleeds to death wide-eyed in a car park. I've given up trying to reintegrate into these peaceful and politically correct societal norms by thinking of serene green meadows the minute one of those violent fantasies emerges from the depths of my subconscious. 'Let me out of here,' were the first words I learned. People expect me to provide oracular pronouncements, perform the devil, the vacuum, string together grown-up words without understanding them. It's mega-tough being an individual. Meeting a child's natural needs. I've never got the slightest kick out of that stuff. I only ever made sandcastles if there was a vague possibility of at least catching the attention of an adult fully equipped with picnic basket and iced tea on the opposite bench in the playground. This impulse is actually the only thing left over from my 'difficult childhood'.

I HAVE NO PROBLEM PROVIDING YOU WITH THE SUBTLE PLEASURES I'VE BEEN DENIED MY WHOLE LIFE LONG, PEOPLE!!

Hail drums against the windows. It's not a light rainfall, it's something that goes right through your bones with dire consequences, the sky dyed dark red, you're sitting in your leather-look multi-media chair, you can't move, and if you get up you'll die.

If the film tears, the world will fall apart.

A thousand monsters cover the surface of the earth, amidst humans rolling in the dirt; they come creeping out of the damp ground and your central nervous system, and while you're still trying to defend yourself you're already bearing their mark on your forehead,

157

enraptured. I'm lying on the ground, letting them stomp me to death. Even now I'm telling lies.

I lie because I actually know very well what I long for. Do you seriously believe, ladies and gentlemen, that I buy into the urgency I've claimed and all the semi-bourgeois bullshit I've written in the past eight months?

I swear I can't believe one word, not one single word of anything I've said in this diary. That is, I believe in the words, I know they correspond to the generally accepted definition of truth, but at the same time it makes me extremely physically uncomfortable to claim it's all justified in some form or other. All the fuss about the fact that the concept of a dog doesn't bark appears to suit me down to the ground. The indignation, the grief about it, even. Hand-made paper has its purposes. Heroin has its purposes too, that goes without saying. Help me, Dostoyevsky!

You're fascinated by your face in the mirror and the way it's toughening up, but it's better you turn to face the wall and don't look at it.

All you motherfucking individuals everywhere out there, all you're interested in is some stupid internship that'll take you to Peking for two semesters, or trying to categorize my dress sense! I'm interested in world wars, severed heads with perfect hairstyles, and not the words, 'Wow, sometimes you wear flares with holes in on Easter Sunday and two days later you turn up in a dress that catapults you and everyone around you straight back to the nineteenth century.'

I'm sitting on a toilet seat, overstressed. The axolotl is hanging from the non-functioning lock mechanism of the toilet cubicle. I'm trying to hold the door closed with one hand, and with the other I key a text to Edmond. I sense I'm REALLY losing my mind, the day has finally come. Come what may.

0:12 a.m. 'Dear Edmond, I just wanted to tell you I love you. You'll probably wonder why now of all times. To be honest I don't really know exactly. I saw that loaf of potato bread in the kitchen today and I thought it had such a cute name and I loved the idea that you went shopping and stood in the bread section and thought, hey, awesome, there's a loaf of bread called Knolli, maybe I should just take that one. It was really yummy too. See you tomorrow. PS: Are they all allowed to be sick? Or presumed dead? Other people's pain already causes me so much pain. Please model your sickness, please do Neuro-Linguistic Programming and please tell everyone to just leave me alone, for fuck's sake.'

'Dear Mifti, my friend Sarah thought you were from the East because you buy ready-sliced cheese.'

When I look around, I'm devastated by the fact there's no toilet paper left. Outside there's a queue of hysterical men; I'm sitting on the men's toilet. 'Hey, babes, go and do your coke somewhere else, we really need to take a dump.'

I haul myself across to the next cubicle and have to explain at great length and in great detail to a bare-chested Swabian of about nineteen that he should go back to Stuttgart right this minute. I'm handed a moisture-soaked toilet roll in return.

By the time I struggle past the queue back into the crowds of people, I'm dizzy, and all of a sudden panic blazes up inside me, a fire licking at the edges of my entire mental life, raging along my throat. OK, that too, I see. Cramped between sweaty faces stuck with red-brown strands of dyed hair, I can certainly imagine something better than falling victim to a panic attack in this atmosphere, of all places.

Every glance shot in my direction transforms into a piercing arrow, and I'm so paranoid that instead of pulling it out I bore it so deeply into my body that no one can see it any more. I line up the steps to be taken next – getting up out of the vodka puddle, tying my soaked shoelaces, heading home or at least getting a breath of night air at a wide-open window. Too blocked; my arms won't move, my knees buckle, my eyes can't focus, and all this with ten-centimetre-long arrows in the region of my ribs, all entangled. I feel like crying but it doesn't work, I feel like remembering what Ophelia said before I took my first ecstasy pill – 'It'll pass' – but that doesn't work either because by now it's not the routine question on the length of the horror, there are just two possibilities lit up dimly ahead of me. Either I survive all this and I can decide tomorrow never to take drugs ever again. I'll write it down on a piece of paper: THAT SHIT'S NO GOOD FOR YOU! And then I can stage an idyllic sex movie sabbatical for three weeks, alternating between pornos and spaghetti alla Sorrentina and parenting books. Or I die right now. Foxy reaches his hand out to me. It costs me a great effort to let him pull me up, lean against the wall for a moment and then stumble three steps to the next opportunity to prop myself up. Which is Alessa. A big red pimple has now emerged under her thick make-up – head-on confrontations with someone else's spots are always rather difficult, of course – and she says, 'Mifti, I'm so sorry about the heroin, shall I stick my finger down your throat?' Someone yells, 'Ha ha, heroin, how out is that?' I know what I want to answer, I open my mouth and my voice fails me, all I can manage is half a nod, which is absolutely exhausting. I manage another four tortuous steps via content-free dancing in a direction not of my choice, and all I can feel is some kind of secreted fluids running down my back. Seven steps until I reach the low banisters around a spiral staircase, where I drag myself up a crazy amount of irregular steps. Someone screams, 'Hey, that girl over there's going up on the roof! Honey, you're not allowed on the roof, they don't let anyone up on the roof after midnight – the likelihood of plunging off drunk is about ninety-nine per cent.'

There's a little skylight at the end of the spiral staircase. I push it open, pulling myself together along with the tiny amount of reserves left in me. Cold wind – it feels as if I am breathing properly for the first time in my life. A three-minute vacation in the Teutoburg Forest. Without consciously experiencing how my body managed it, I find myself finally standing on two firm legs, right in the middle of the roof, taking in a deeply moving view across Berlin. I instantly discover three burning rubbish bins in the west of the city. When I turn around I see a small group of people shaking each other's hands at a distance of about a hundred yards. One figure breaks off and moves in my direction in a starkly familiar rhythm. The shape of her handbag is starkly familiar too. The sound of her heels is starkly familiar. She's still too fit to walk on the balls of her feet.

Suddenly she's standing before me at a competently maintained distance, raising one slow hand and running it through her hair on the left and right, and I can't help laughing; it's so typical of her. And different from how she used to be. It's as if I were meeting her for the first time all over again, even though she's her. In two thousand different countries, in two thousand apartments, in hell, in heaven – she'll always be her.

I look at her, she looks at me. We stand there like two squirrels in a cartoon, suddenly realizing in the middle of a bush that the entire outside world can be ignored with a clear conscience. No idea how long. My sense of time is overshadowed by something else. It might be two minutes' silence or two hours'. In any case, it's all incredible; the sweat on my skin turns into a layer of ice sheathing my entire body. My face turns to stone and my mouth hangs open. Alice. OK. I've already started to find it stylish to hype you as a long-lost legend, and now suddenly you're standing right here staring at me, just when my regeneration phase has finally kicked in, and my heart rate is forced to return to normal territory.

'Have you hurt yourself?' she says.
    'Pardon?'
    'Someone or other trips over the last step about thirty times a night. I heard moaning and I thought, shit, not again.'
    DEAR GOD, I'M NOT ASKING HER TO FOR-SAKE HER INTRANSPARENCY, ALL I'M ASKING FOR IS A TEENY WEENY BIT OF FREEDOM!!!!!!
    'Was I moaning?'
    'You were making some kind of noise.'
    'It's all just a bit much for me.'
    'Yeah, I get that a lot too.'

162

'I know.'

'Err . . .'

'Why are you like that?'

'I think you're running a fever, is everything all right?'

'What on earth is supposed to be all right?'

'Honey?'

'It's nothing.'

'That's just what I wanted to hear.'

'I'd better ask you what you're doing here then.'

'DJing. In ten minutes. So if you want a drink you'll have to tell me NOW.'

'No.'

'Mifti?'

'Yes?'

She takes a breath and that's just what I've been waiting for, for that tiny spark of honesty in her face, for her every movement to take place in slow motion, for time to stand still in some way and for us to look at each other again and know that what's happened so far and every drink and every job are all suddenly utterly meaningless.

'Do you despise me?'

And then something suddenly overcomes me.

'Remember how you showed me the ocean? When I was sick in that holiday home in France with waves of fever, between all those over-dimensional animal posters and photos of sunsets in frameless glass frames, you know what I'm getting at, when I got in that panic and had a forty-degree temperature. I know now why that was. I was scared of my own body or the fact that my consciousness has nothing to do with the world, let alone with my flesh or my skin and all the material you can see on the surface, just allocated to me like it always had been. I wanted to give up thinking because words were meaningless, because meaninglessness was meaningless, because my life wasn't worth anything, because my entire physiognomy is part of the inherently consistent organism of a populated celestial body from which I keep distancing myself. And then you walked to the ocean with me in the morning. Every morning we stared at the ocean and we loved being there because it was like us, Alice. It was the answer to everything. That ocean was obvious. And oceans are only oceans when they move. Everything you asked me and everything we saw and did, it was all obvious, it was a work of art, and that artwork was us.

'Oceans are just their waves and every wave breaks at some point, simply because it moves forwards. I keep seeing your face and how it moves into some expression. The waves that break lose their shape in a gesture that expresses that shape in the first place. And now, now you're suddenly standing right here. And I can see your face, but in some different way. And I can't even imagine you really exist any more.'

Not turning around to me again, she climbs back through the skylight, the personification of business casual wear. Or more like the personification of flirtation. I have never in my life trembled as uncontrollably as now. My star-spangled sky, my Berlin, my total collapse reminiscent of an epileptic attack.

Despite it all, I somehow manage to fulfil the most rudimentary demand made of party guests: if you can't be cool, at least be inconspicuous. If this was a film there'd be a camera fastened above my head using some special construction, plummeting vertically towards me every time I breathed in. A tear would roll down my cheek and torrential rain would set in. In the most extreme case, they might tell me to do something completely insane, maybe empty a champagne glass over myself and screech, 'OK, here we go, now I'm gonna fuck you!' But sadly, the world doesn't work like that, I realize at the very last moment.

0:24 a.m. Emre is just mixing his last two tracks, and Alice puts down her record case all covered in stickers, takes off her coat, gives him a brief hug and puts on her headphones. Ophelia comes over to me in tears. I tell her, 'Your father would be really glad if he knew you were partying tonight, I bet.'

She slaps me round the face. How I've missed that numb feeling that comes after a slap. I hit her back.

'WHAT DO YOU REALLY WANT ANYWAY, MIFTI? HUH? ALICE IS HERE, WHY DON'T YOU JUST GET CHATTING ABOUT GREAT RAPE FILMS AGAIN AT LAST?'

'The thing with ALICE is a thing about music and nothing else. About everything in the world. And nothing. It's nothing to do with homosexuality.'

She slaps me again and says with an expression solidifying into ultimate disgust, 'Jesus, you are disgusting.' I'm not even registering properly any more, so all I can do is give an idiotic laugh and let someone drag me away. It's the guy in the motto sweatshirt.

'FUCK YOU, MIFTI! FUCK YOU! FUCK OFF AND DIE, I NEVER WANT TO SEE YOU AGAIN!'

'What's up with you two?' asks the motto sweatshirt guy, and seeing as I don't respond he adds, 'Is everything OK?'

'No, absolutely nothing is OK.'

'Well, that's a starting point at least.'

'Where's my axolotl? My axolotl's gone, can you help me find my axolotl? It was here a minute . . .' and then I break off mid-sentence, because I identify the first guitar chords initiated by Alice as a song just for me. None of the wedding guests are into The Zombies. Into creatures trapped between life and death and performing 'She's Not There' in a serious state of underfucked love. The situation on the simulated dance floor alters drastically, but she does her thing as hard as nails.

I say, 'It's all so obvious.'

The guy, now stuck to my back, has dumped me down in front of a trestle table laden with flowers and wedding presents. The axolotl is floating sadly in a glass bowl full of water. He says, 'Oh shit, look, is this real?'

I look at the gun in his hand. He's just picked it up from the table. A fat bald guy comes towards us from behind, just as Colin Blunstone is singing, *But it's too late to say you're sorry, how would I know, why should I care?*

'It's not only real, it's a nine-millimetre semi-automatic pistol and next to it is a loaded spare cartridge.'

'It's loaded?'

I'm like, 'Put it away please.'

'Has Albrecht seen it yet? Why did you give him something like this?'

> *Well, no one told me about her*
> *The way she lied*
> *No one told me about her*
> *How many people cried*

'What kind of question is that?'

'What kind of signals are you trying to give off, huh? That married men have to shoot themselves? Or someone

166

else? Mifti, get your axolotl right now, we've got to get out of here.'

'All right, I will, although actually . . .?'

Ah but don't go home with your hard-on . . .
You can't melt it down in the rain You can't melt it
down in the rain You can't melt it down in the rain
You can't melt it down in the rain
(Leonard Cohen)

I wake up in a child's pale blue bedroom, which has a door that leads into a back garden through glass panes. On the ornate plastic bedside table next to me is a small white piece of paper. I can't yet summon up enough energy to decipher what it says. I get up and walk through a maisonette apartment ripped off from some alternative parenting magazine, instantly identifiable as requiring 5,000 euro a month net income. In the bathroom I hang my weak head under the tap, gulp down three litres of water and then lie down in the empty bathtub to wait for it to fill up. After, wrapped up in a towel, I position myself in front of the mirror for the first time in three days; I've almost forgotten what I look like. Then I lie down under the covers again with wet hair and read the note: *Stay in bed as long as you like, everything's fine.*

The motto sweatshirt guy appears in the doorway dressed only in boxer shorts and says, 'Stay in bed as long as you like, everything's fine.'

He really does look kinda good, like a guy in a nouvelle vague film set on a sailing boat. They have this special kind of biceps that I just can't help admiring; it has nothing to do with rowing machines, it's purely genetic.

'What time is it?'

'Five a.m.'

'Have I only slept that long?'

'You went to sleep at three the night before last and you've slept through till now. You've missed a whole day of your life. Hold on, I'll show you something.' He bangs around the flat and comes back with a photo album open on his mobile phone. My pupils jump out at me from the screen, the size of plates on that ketamine night two weeks ago. It's scary and I tell him so. Then we introduce each other. His name is Viktor and he won't tell me what he does for a living. On the basis of my burnt-out behaviour the night before last, he's decided I'm intelligent enough to work it out for myself. 'I don't want to get into your pants, by the way. I'm not really interested in you. I think you're objectively hot, if you get what I mean, but I'm absolutely not interested in you.'

'You're a psychotherapist!'

'Spot on.'

'And you hang out, extremely well-dressed, in some practice on Kollwitzplatz with red velvet curtains.'

'Spot on.'

'I went to one of those once. In the end the therapist said I was therapy-resistant and I had to drag myself out with a numb leg that had gone to sleep. It was so incredibly embarrassing. A numb leg and smudged eyeliner. He's like, "Are you all right?" And I'm like, "Yeah, sure, my leg's just gone to sleep, oh God."'

'OK?'

169

'And with the second therapist it was like, OK, he was supposed to be the absolute über-dude of a therapist, so anyway, I go in there and I see a Heidegger book and I crank up the precociousness and say, "Oh, Heidegger!" And he answers, "Hey, if you think I'm gonna chat philosophy with you, you've got another thing coming." The third one chucked me out at some point and three days later there was this all-blue postcard in the mail saying she was sorry, something came over her. And the fourth one wanted me to draw a person, a tree and a road before she even introduced herself. My father had one too. I was supposed to go along with him one time. She was really, really abysmal. Classic case of counter-transference. She talked to me about my truancy issues for a couple of minutes, and my dad fell asleep on the chair opposite me.'

A child of four at the most with a Playboy bunny shaved into the back of her head is standing in the room. 'We could play with my pyramid,' she says.

Viktor says in a really cool, laid-back tone of voice, 'Hey, come on, either you go back to sleep or you keep yourself occupied for a while.' And I realize there is a world that exists without expensive viscose fabric samples or the constantly repeated statement, 'Three days after my first arsefuck I discovered a fingertip of lube cream on the end of my log.'

'But Papa, I don't know what to play.'

'I can't help it if there's no diamond castle on offer for a change and only your enormous collection of educational toys, but please stop being so annoying! Boredom can be a great thing once in a while. I've got three different options for you, but we can't do any of them for at least two hours. You can either tidy your room—'

'But there's someone in my bed.'

'Never mind that. Would you be willing to tidy your room?'

'No way. Hey, what is there to tidy up?'

'Your train tracks, for example, and then you can sort out all your different frogs.'

'What's the second option?'

'Mifti makes waffles with you. Sorry, Mifti.'

'And the third one?'

'You go back to sleep now, and afterwards I'll read you the story about the pig that wouldn't wash. There's this pig that refuses to take a bath, and then one day it does have a bath and it never wants to get out again because it's so great. And after that I'll read you that other book, the one that explains what all the different kinds of tractors do.'

'Why such crap books?'

'Because you chose them yesterday, Bibi.'

Then we all sit there with gelatinous milk chocolate mush in our mouths and alternate between discussing German splatter films, Madonna's biceps and therapy programmes.

'When I was a twenty-six-year-old student I was so broke that I put a small ad in the paper, with a female friend of mine. We called ourselves "Amor and Psyche", that was kind of hip back then, and we advised men with no sex lives on the broad subject of women for fifty euro an hour.'

'Like consultant physicians?'

'Yup. Oh, er, hmmm, maybe you should try this one: not wearing clothes.'

171

'And then?'

'It was a complete nightmare, we'd be sitting there with these unattractive consultant physicians and persuading them, hey, if you can get a woman to talk about her childhood, that means she's in love with you.'

'Well, I was raped as a child.'

'Oh really?'

'No. The whole rape thing's just supposed to relativize the fact that I still expect anything from that disgusting bastard. I love the guy. He's not the only person I love, but he might be the only one I can still believe in, surrounded by all this stupid out-of-touch shit here. So. And then I had a mother too until not that long ago. Very simple issue: she was schizophrenic, obsessive-compulsive, neurotic, sadistic, highly intelligent and unemployable because of the drugs. We lived in a one-bedroom flat and shared a bed every night until she died. Whenever I woke up in the morning and she wasn't lying next to me, I knew she'd be stretched out over the kitchen table, totally melancholy and drunk as a skunk with her head buried in her arms. I get home, she's lying around somewhere – that's how our peaceful coexistence worked for the main part. Putting up with her corporal punishment was a relatively bearable state of affairs, because then our roles were clearly defined and my position was clear-cut: just being the weak one for a change. I read this book a while back about co-dependency but I couldn't find an explanation model that fitted me. They analysed all these different family combinations, but drug-addict single parents with only children between three and thirteen simply don't come up. In view of all that, I can say, yes, I went through some stuff back then, and now I'm starting to ask myself how I managed it. But unfortunately it didn't make me into a great artist. It's really kind of difficult for me. All that getting tortured. It switches off your dissociation, your ability to adapt; a person like that can't get used to physical pain.'

'It's amazing that you can talk about it.'

'See? That's what I was going for, that one bastard sentence that I never wanted to hear again. It doesn't make any difference whether I talk about it or not. I've been repeating myself for three years, in this glitter, dirt and sequin system, a real bad nightmare bass for grown-ups. I can't stand it. I have no problem talking about anything that's ever happened to me that entails post-traumatic disorders, but you know, it's a total myth that it's possible to get your head around all your personal issues with all that psychology crap. It doesn't get you anywhere. Regardless of that, what you can say is, I'll be disabled for the rest of my life and no one can change that. I'll be able to understand the behaviour of suicide bombers for the rest of my life, and no one can change that.'

'Yes, maybe.'

'I have a whole load of raised scars to show off as soon as anyone accuses me of social incompetence or anything else, and then they leap up like enchanted ambulance-chasers – the whole deadly dull mass of psychologists, constantly maintaining something curdled into general understanding – and then they say, oh, what did they do to you, how great that you can talk about it, then maybe you'll finally be normal soon. And that cements me right back into the victim maze, while all the others stumble out triumphantly somewhere or other. Every single second, you have to remember to conform to some norm or other and slave away at some stupid convention crap or other. She abandoned me once, when I was about sixteen months old. And everyone says you can't remember that far back, but I remember that feeling, of being abandoned, and in a way being killed to some extent as well. Can you imagine how mega-aggressive I am to all the pseudo-experienced bastards all around me, who've never been confronted with any serious difficulty except maybe rheumatism or a broken heart? And then they want to tell me what to do in life and what's acceptable and what's not and what's OK from an artistic point of view and that you must never talk about that kind of subject in a socially critical singsong, because that's repulsive and out and everything has to take place on a totally sober and best of all entertaining level or best of all not at all, because it's not even a social taboo, all it is is kitsch. I'm always thinking no – you have no idea of anything except orderly conditions, and as soon as your conditions aren't orderly, if they're not neat and tidy like they ought to be then you just take a brief jaunt through some kind of drug hell or you go to wild parties or puke all down your nineteen-forties Gucci dress, and that's that, you go straight back to your tagliatelle. I hate people. Apart from Bibi, she's great, I've just noticed. She's sitting over there, throwing specially designed pharaohs off Playmobil cliffs, and she doesn't ask too much. Modest and unassuming. Top of the pops.'

'Did they even have Gucci in the Forties?'

'Sorry?'

'Are you in love with anyone right now?'

'Yes, you can tell, can't you? I'm in love with someone who said things to me that I've started dreaming about now. Every night. Shit. Now I've really gone and turned into one of those melodramatic weeping Wendys just because the woman happens to be perverted. And then I had a row with my best friend the day before yesterday. If the worst comes to the worst, she'll write and tell me she'll always love me and she can tell by my eyes where I've been and she's my witness. And then we'll never see each other again. We've always argued, once just because I made her a mix-tape and that offended her honour as a music expert, but this time it's different somehow. None of it matters anyway.'

'Shall we have another lie-down?'

'Yes.'

Then we lie on his bed side by side, while outside lots of friendly little people go to work or eat cream cheese bagels. Just before I fall asleep he says, 'Turn around a bit, I want to show you something.' And when I turn around he just puts his arm around me, in that decisive banker's manner you see in films occasionally, and then I fall asleep, and when I wake up for a moment in between, I put my arm around him for a change, and then I fall asleep again. The whole thing ends up with his head between my legs and me screaming in ecstasy and tossing and turning from left to right and digging my hands into his elbows as he props himself up on the bed.

At some point I force myself to get up. As I'm tiptoeing to the front door I spot an aquarium lined with large pebbles on top of a cabinet in the hall. Estimated gross water capacity, 160 litres. It has to be lighter in the aquarium during the day than at night, and that just about sums up the axolotl's needs in terms of lighting concepts. If there was ever a more idyllic moment in the history of my personal heteromatrix or at least in the history of humankind, then I've never heard about it.

From: Ophelia
To: Mifti
Subject: Day before day before yesterday

'That's my childhood, the childhood of an orphan, a found-
ling, a homeless little girl with no father or mother, who
never had love bestowed upon her. It was awful, but I have
no regrets.' And then she said, 'Prettiness fades, beauty
remains.' What terrible thing did you send me, it made me
want to puke – animal masks are totally in right now,
non-stop animal masks, expressionless potato fields everywhere you look and expressionless people in animal masks.
The two of us can be so unbeatable together and stir up the
whole crappy little pessimistic leftist cultural scene so bad it
makes them all break out in a sweat. I know all the tricks, I
just haven't used any of them yet.

You have to tell me what your songs are called so I can use
them on my life.

From: Mifti
To: Ophelia
Subject: RE: Day before day before yesterday

(I-now-because everyone's stopped doing
    culture-think-doing a bit of
        art-wouldn't do me any harm as the
            idiots' mainstream arrogance is suddenly
            befalling us, the lower
middle class has it's parents' money – so we could
        almost . . . be like Oscar
        Wilde wrote . . . are you down with me? guess so)

176

are you flattering me? aren't we experts at that?
don't I know all the tricks?
   is hate love hate and hate love or love despite
      precisely because nevertheless or simply
   it isn't
   simple

PS: Just to get one thing straight: there's nothing you can give me in terms of music that I don't yet have, don't already know. And darling, there is no generally accepted hierarchy that covers all aspects of life. That's a classic German fallacy. Of course you're miles above me, but you know that already. I'm less than existent in German culture. But I don't care about that. I'll just let you have your world and you let me have mine.

From: Mifti
To: Ophelia
Subject: RE: RE: Day before day before yesterday

You've adapted to set patterns of thinking and feeling because you've internalized norms. That's your personality structure and that's carved in stone for the most part.

Not that I care. I don't know what to say to you, honestly.

From: Ophelia
To: Mifti
Subject: RE: RE: RE: Day before day before yesterday

My dear, I'm really not made to worship other people – even you – how can you think something like that? Why should one person be above another person? What criteria is that based on? Let me assure you, I'm a long way down in your ranking system. Personality structure? Since when has anything like that existed and why should personality be static?

OK, I'm not fucking German and I do not understand half of your way of thinking *BUT*, Jesus, how dare you think that music is received by me just the same way as it is by hundreds of other people? That was insulting. Well, it's the internet and it's easy. Press delete or ignore – what the hell did you think I had to offer you?

Let's just not talk about music, OK? What norms have I internalized? Saying that's just a phrase, and phrases are way below your level. Also, I'd really be interested in what my structure looks like, that one that's carved in stone. Because you're the first person who's ever been able to define it in words. What do you want? To keep me?

From: Ophelia
To: Mifti
Subject: RE: RE: RE: RE: Day before day before yesterday

Yes, of course.

From: Pörksen
To: Mifti
Subject: (no subject)

Sorry, Mifti, we didn't really talk properly at the wedding – just wanted to get back to you on the subject of that thing again. You're plagued by existential fears? Man, hey, YOU'RE the one plaguing the EXISTENTIAL FEARS! I messed up. I'm a baaaastard, I know. But seeing as we've had the same kind of missing each other so many times the other way round, and seeing as you love me, just like I love you (and dammit, I do!), I know you will and must forgive me. Yup, it's as simple as that, honey-bun (goddammit!). Shall we go to Stadtbad tonight? Or to Arm und Sexy. Or we could have a grog together at lunchtime or eat mince. I'm at the office, the only dumb thing is I forgot my telephone so you can only get me via thingy, you know.

From: Ophelia
To: Mifti
Subject: RE: RE: RE: RE: RE: Day before day before
          yesterday

That's easily said. And you know it.

Dear Holy Saint Mifti, in view of yesterday's situation I started wondering what you expect from me. To look old and ugly next to you? To admire you unconditionally?

I have to ask you again, how can you not have noticed that I'm not made to worship other people? You've had enough experience out there! And I'm not some insignificant direc-tor's 46-year-old ex-girlfriend who you want to manipulate.

All I'm getting at is that I want you to allow me something that makes me me. I feel like we're in an 'anything you can do I can do better' situation. Of course you get more confirmation, because I'm a complete coward and I hoard files of photos and texts and music on my computer and under the bed. Because I create extreme amounts of stuff and then lose interest in it as soon as it's finished, which actually corresponds to the idea of art, that if it's a question of art or life, I'm always shouting out: both – and please, what's the difference if you mean it seriously. Your family said art, mine said money. And now, as you can imagine, I'm annoyed that it's all lying around somewhere not making any profit.

I ask myself three things: are you worth all the effort and why should I ever go anywhere with you ever again and apart from that, how inflationary is your use of compliments, in actual fact?

Sometimes I wish I knew how you'd insult me, then I'd know what's the worst thing to expect from you – and that's not psycho, it's strategic.

I'm so dissociative that I can turn into what other people see in me, so I'm sure you'll allow me to ask a couple of questions before I transform into a forty-year-old wreck just to make you happy.

I'm fantastically socially compatible, as long I don't care about the people I'm dealing with. If you say so, I'll keep Saturday free, but if I end up hanging around and waiting and don't hear from you, then I won't do anything with you again.

And if you're gone now, you're gone. Better now than later, when you've got used to someone.

I'm sooo tired, Mifti, I'm tired and dumb and sad and I'm just scared that the little bit I have will end up halved and halved to infinity, and nothing will be left of me.

From: Mifti
To: Ophelia
Subject: RE: RE: RE: RE: RE: RE: Day before day before
yesterday

I means love nothing else.

From: Mifti
To: Ophelia
Subject: RE: RE: RE: RE: RE: RE: Day before day before
yesterday

I means: it means love nothing else.

From: Mifti
To: Ophelia
Subject: RE: RE: RE: RE: RE: RE: Day before day before
yesterday

Meant.

16th June

I can't walk straight any more. The train arrives quite blurred, and it's boiling hot inside. We take off our sweatshirt jackets and grab four seats facing each other. There are all these super-micro-families in endless variations of checked shirts around us, making like they're really 'touched' as soon as their gaze inevitably falls on me. So I'm sitting there, an insane emptiness in my head, everything's kind of all right, and only the whites of my eyes are visible, so to speak. My pupils keep drifting off the whole time. Everything, happens, like, kinda.

Then at some point a park bench. Edmond, Annika and me staring bombed out of our brains at a couple of bunny rabbits by the tree opposite us. Funnily enough, I expect a yielding crack as my skull is shattered by something like a baseball bat and I tip over. There've been no sounds for a while now anyway. I give a wail of pain, grab my head and crawl around on the grass, yelling through the litter on the ground, I breathe out, and bright white smoke rolls along a neat sandy path, disappearing in the shadow of the tree and coming back to us a moment later, until we're wrapped in a lead-grey cloud. Crazy weather, by the way, I think it might be Sunday, Wednesday at most. A group of women in bright pink sports outfits jog past us, laughing. My mobile rings. Edmond and Annika give each other a kind of funny look, and when my father pipes up on the other end and says, 'Kiddo, I have to read you something!' another paranoia attack struggles to the surface.

'What?'

'They knocked out the old stove in the bedroom yesterday, the whole flat's covered in dust sheets and someone knocked over a bucket of rubble. Anyway, on the wall behind the stove, where that huge picture of the forest used to be, there are all these old newspapers from 1960, and it says, "To Yuri Gagarin, USSR – congratulations on your great achievement! Humankind has always dreamed of flying into space!"'

'Ah, that's sweet.'

'Do you want to come round for a bit?'

We don't say a single word on the way to our father's place. We haven't exchanged one word all day long, but suddenly the silence isn't the result of pure boredom, it's something else; something more unnerving. As if the other two were in on a plot against me, and it's giving them a guilty conscience.

The builders have left the flat in a very, very bad state. Franziska's wearing a white T-shirt and invites us in with a pseudo-relaxed gesture. I want to go to the toilet but my father's standing naked at the basin with his back to me and says, 'Can you wait outside a minute?'

I say, 'Dental floss in the bathroom is actually totally unsexy, but camouflaged as a shark like that it looks kind of decorative.'

We've been through some pretty strange situations in this atmosphere. Our last family get-together started with a Patti Smith cover version of 'Gimme Shelter' and ended with us rushing outside without saying goodbye. My father was enthroned on one of his rococo furnishings with his back to us, staring at the TV tower through the wall of windows. So now we're back here again. Nirvana, just like the old days. Here we are now, entertain us, yeah, that's right. Something suddenly stops buzzing. Either the light or the wasp trapped in the window frame.

I'm offered a seat on the sofa in a mega-formal manner. I'm starting to notice more and more clearly with every second how sober and upset this family is acting. Franziska with her fear-instilling horsey teeth is hanging on a chair, her torso leant forward in a mega-opportunist pose, a permanent nervous grin on her face. She's put on the hand-me-down Sabrina Dehoff scarf I gave her. My father's staring at a table leg, his fingers spread and affixed to his mouth, Annika's smoking, and Edmond looks me in the eye without laughing for the first time in his life. So they start off talking about how they all find it difficult to distinguish between the terms signifier and signified. I say I mainly find it difficult to distinguish between DIY stores and electronics stores, but nobody laughs. In fact nobody here has laughed at all during the past half hour. 'Hey, I was really loving that!' I say, for no reason other than desperation.

Annika says in a pretty bored voice, 'Who did that come from again?'

'From Consti, when he was bouncing.'

Dad, 'Bouncing?'

'At that thing in Munich last year, when he shouted down the stairs, "Hey, guys, they're playing hip-hop!"

And we like totally bounced for six hours in a row, and later we were in a taxi, Consti was at the front and Timo and me were in the back, and he turns round and says, "Hey, I was really loving that!"'

'Ha ha.'

'He was deadly serious and we were like, "Awesome, yeah."'

'Awesome, yeah.'

'Mifti, we . . .'

'Yes?'

'Mifti, I have to, actually—'

'Don't say anything, Dad.'

'But—'

'Please just don't say anything, all right?'

Annika: 'Mifti?'

I sense strong waves of energy pulsing through me. I feel movement. Enormous, increasing movement. When I look around, shapes form out of the blur. I'm facing four people radiating sensationalism and sadism. Every pore of their bodies seems to be radiating light. The group gathers around the dining table and I know it's time for me to sit down.

'Mifti, look at us. We know you've got massive problems.'

'Why the hell do you think you have the right to claim you know the slightest thing about ME?'

'We're not talking about dope or truancy here.'

'So what are we talking about?'

'You're mortally unhappy.'

'Did you read that in the book *Why Our Kids Are Turning into Dirty Sex Beasts?*'

'No.'

'Do you ever read parenting books? Do you

sometimes get so bored and sentimental that you read those instant parenting instruction manuals, and now you think you ought to fulfil some duty sixteen years on by telling me I'm mortally unhappy? Do I get an answer?'

'Honey, I'm really sorry about this, but . . . Edmond?'

Edmond rummages in his bag, pulling something out in slow motion, and I see that it's a magenta notebook with my name written on the cloth binding.

Mifti: you losers.

They've got everything I wrote in their hands there, and I feel like I don't even exist any more. I close my eyes, and as I rotate around my own axis I'm suddenly detached from my body as a cloud-like empty hull, no idea how that happens all of a sudden, and I watch everything that takes place from above. I see my body screaming and I feel how that scream drives into me. How I try to resist with all my strength, but it must be some kind of incomprehensible detachment from my model of myself. I'm just about to enter a state of non-existence.

My body tears the notebook out of Edmond's hands and runs to the door. Edmond grabs my arm and says, 'I'll say one thing for you.'

'What?'

The words bring us back into a single entity, my body and me – odd.

'You write like roadkill.'

'Like what?'

'Like a dead animal squashed against the road.'

I slam the door behind me and count my money. The necessity of a family is just dissolving before my very eyes. Mummy, Daddy, baby – why can't we wipe out this barbaric family model at long last? The only way out is spilling blood and guts. Or, as in my case, getting yourself disowned in a terribly tragic drama. Despite our blood ties to each other, I've suddenly managed to hand in my notice. I haven't got a sister any more, or a brother, or a father. You need more than goodwill for a community to work. Goodwill towards the model doesn't mean the model will work. I get on a random bus and spend all day riding around, seeing as I have no destination whatsoever. Seeing as I have to start a new chapter. I watch myself discovering a new existence, or whatever you want to call it, when suddenly the word *heroin* lights up and you get off the bus without even noticing at Kottbusser Tor station, the epicentre of Berlin's illegal drug supply chain, eyed by a one-legged old biddy who does look a bit scary despite it all – and in the end I send Ophelia the last text she's ever going to get from me, asking for the number of her nineteen-year-old Russian from the organic waste bin. She sends me his contact details at 16:42 with no further comment. Say whatever you want, scream at me, shove me up against the walls, beat me out of bed, stare me in the eyes or laugh at me – I can't do anything to change it. I can't watch you lying to me. Watch you pretending you want me to do nothing.

What do I want?

I want you to laugh, to cry, to know what you've got before it's gone. I don't want you to think you're on your own, I want you to be free, to come to me, to stop forgetting everything, not to have to do anything, to want to do something, to try new things, to leave me behind. If you have to.

* * *

At 22:00 I check into the Ibis Hotel on Prenzlauer Allee, so bored that I wash my clothes with soap in the basin and watch repeats of docusoaps all night long, which is great because in one of them there's this fourteen-year-old girl whose father collects vintage cars and her mother has a poodle farm with four apricot-coloured king poodles and two white ones. They all live together in this completely tumbledown house in the East German countryside, and naturally enough the daughter Justine is pretty pissed off because her parents' time-consuming hobbies mean they not only neglect their household duties, they also neglect her. But most of all Justine gets upset about all the dog turds in the living room, which stop her from ever inviting friends round.

> How the rare times when a vicissitude of human relating, sheep-shearing, or pasture-status pissed him off, he'd get positively other-, under-worldly with anger, a bearded unit of pure and potent rage, ranging his sheep's ranges like something mythopoeic, thunderous, less man or thing than sudden and dire force, will, ill.
> *(David Foster Wallace)*

I walk round the Galeries Lafayette and deposit all the cashmere sweaters I come across in my bag as conspicuously as possible, as befits my current state of mind. The ones that don't fit in pile up on my folded arms. Then I take a long detour to the exit via various escalators. Naturally enough, the electronic security device starts bleeping. Perfectly aware of the faked school ID card in my pocket, I stop and wait for the store detective, who comes running up behind me and grabs me coyly by the arm.

Half an hour later, I'm at a police station in the company of two of those curly-permed policewomen straight out of an early-evening TV series. One of them is staring at one of the two computers and taking down my details.

I keep repeating the sentence, 'My name's Ophelia and I'm thirteen years old.'

'Nothing will happen to you anyway then.'

I show her the fake school ID.

'Haven't you got a proper ID card?'

'You don't have one when you're thirteen.'

'Oh, right.'

'What do you want to be when you grow up?'

'A policewoman.'

'Sounds interesting.'

'YOU'RE telling ME that?'

'You'll ruin your future if you keep stealing three hundred euros' worth of clothes and getting caught. A parent or guardian has to come and collect you, otherwise we can't let you go. Can we get hold of one of your parents?'

'Well . . .'

'What? Your father? Your mother? Is neither of them available?'

'My father's putting on a ready-made opera in Brazil right now.'

'And your mother? Huh?'

'She's in a psychiatric hospital.'

'Oh.'

'But, well, there's a friend of the family who's kind of . . .'

'Kind of . . . ?'

'Been awarded . . .'

'Kind of.'

'. . . my CUSTODY.'

And that's the moment I've been waiting for since all that excess on the coast of France. I text Alice.

A heavily armed police officer comes in, shakes hands with the two women and, after a brief hesitation, with me. Then he disappears again.

'Look how fast you've climbed the career ladder, Ophelia. Now they think you're an intern.'

I've been waiting ninety minutes. I hear Alice's voice in the corridor, leap up and walk to meet her. Alice is having a discussion with the doorman about the correct hardness of wood for chopping. When she sees me she stares at me in disbelief for a moment, until a cautious smile gradually takes possession. She rushes towards me, sweeping me up in an embrace and saying demonstratively over my shoulder to one of the policewomen: 'Baby, what's all this crap you're getting up to, huh?' I don't take my eyes off the floor.

'The child really doesn't have it easy with all that garbled art crap and the tiny little flat and six younger siblings and hardly any pocket money. It won't happen again, will it, Mifti?'

'What won't happen again?'

'Mifti? Why Mifti?'

'You know, the criminal activity stuff.'

'Mifti, yeah, that's what Alice always calls me because she finds my real name crap, depressing, oppressive, crap, umm . . .'

'Can you sign here please?'

'Exactly, depressing, oppressive, crap.'

'Like a slap in the face for the soul, ha ha.'

'Oh, I don't care.'

'Sign where? Here?'

'Yes, right here where my finger is, that's it.'

'So, right, here.'

'Where my finger is. Thanks very much.'

No no, no no no no, no no no no no
(Roy Orbison)

She's working this ultra-chic neo-folk look. A jungle-green velour leather biker jacket, an oversized cardigan and a Donna Karan bag with a double zip for 1,543 euros, as in: city girls know that an across-the-body bag's the only way to keep your essentials in one place at the height of summer.

Her hair's kind of blowing in the wind – what else is it supposed to do in this situation? – and we're walking side by side along a pavement with a startling amount of plant growth.

'Can't you nick tights from H&M like any normal girl your age? Does it have to be that secretary chic? Ophelia? OPHELIA? WHY THE HELL DID YOU THINK UP SUCH A STUPID BLOODY NAME FOR YOUR-SELF?'

'Can you help me?'

'WHAT WITH?' she shouts really loudly.

'I can't go home.'

'Sweetheart, it's—'

'I don't know what to do, really. I can envisage one of those nasty wood-panelled institutional short-term homes where you have to share a room with four under-achieving bulimics under the age of eighteen and do basket-weaving and take part in video-supported therapy groups sitting on beanbags. All I can do right now is accidentally kick in windscreens from the passenger seat, and then all this shattered glass shit rains down on me.'

Take the money and run
(Steve Miller)

'Really.'

'Or you can (. . .)'

'I keep demolishing stuff the whole time.'

'You can . . .'

'It's all just really crap right now, Alice, it's all just really badly crap right now.'

'MIFTI, DO YOU WANT TO SLEEP AT MY PLACE?'

Now she starts blubbing, in all seriousness, from one second to the next there's a blend of mascara and tears flooding down her face, and to make it worse I know why. I don't react, standing still due to a psychosomatic dizziness attack and propping myself up against some lamp post. This thing here right now: I think it's equivalent to seeing my own face reflected in the creation of the world. From one second to the next, this woman no longer matches up to my image of her. Maybe because I know that I don't match up to her image of me any more. That I'm too old now – I can tell by her face. I can only rely on the idea that this impulse to turn around and leave is a mistake. That she hasn't changed, and that everything will work just like it used to. And that's why I nod.

'You can sleep at my place, it's no problem.'

We get into a red Mercedes with a white leather interior. All I know is that she always used to say she didn't have a driving licence. Maybe she really hasn't got one. But she's obviously got herself a new Mercedes. We bomb silently through the shit in it, listening to Brinsley Schwarz on repeat from a mix CD of seventies stuff.

The sky darkens. She parks outside a rococo building, closer to the Turkish part of Schöneberg than the gay part and only a hundred yards away from one of the two branches of Lidl with the best opening hours in the city. I wind the window down and watch her walking through the front door into a corridor with black wood and mirrors. I don't dare to ask where she's going and how long she'll be gone. Just after the twenty-two tracks have played all the way through for the second time and the street lights have switched on, Alice comes back with her face washed. She gets back in the car and looks at me.

I'm like, 'Where were you?'

'I cancelled my lover.'

'And how am I supposed to react to that?'

'Not at all.'

She takes a new CD out of the glove compartment and puts it in the player, takes a deep breath, clutches the steering wheel and says, as she stares straight ahead through the windscreen without blinking a single time, 'What do you do when the war's over?'

I shrug my shoulders. 'What war do you mean?'

'That doesn't matter. You put on an old raincoat and wipe the dirt off your face, you walk through the rain to the end of the platform at a small-town station, from where you can see the grey ocean. You put your bag on the black, battered train standing there as if it had been expecting you. You sit down on a seat made of first-class leather, it smells totally musty and mouldy, and you stare through the yellowed train curtains at the wheels just chugging their dumb rotating rhythm. Your state of mind begins to improve as you speed through a landscape of metal and concrete. Through a dilapidated world that seems permanently on the brink of collapsing forever. Dirty washing hangs in ash-pale backyards, abandoned toys everywhere, they're all wilted impressions, and your concentrated face is framed, so to speak, by a window to the past that you're constantly trying to fold up forever. On your withdrawal to some place called home that's still a long way away at the moment. And where fearful encounters await you, hopefully a cup of tea, warmth, sleep. I think all that would sound a bit like this.'

She presses Play. Let's just go home, I think. Curled up small in the passenger seat, I start to cry and don't stop for a long time. Because I've found it. Because this is true love and true hate and true revulsion and real disappointment.

Machine Gun
(Portishead)

She lives in a plasterboard palace in a converted loft space. The apartment is primarily cream. Mega-old tables, mega-old seating opportunities and expensive picture frames. I sit down in the kitchen. We drink some kind of nasty tea, made of leaves that turned yellow when she poured water on them. I don't dare raise the cup to my lips, knowing full well I'll drop it:

I lie down on her bed, absolutely terrified. It's one long moment of expectation.

I sit up, she leans down to me and says, 'You've changed.'

I say, 'You changed me.'

I kneel on the floor. My wrists are crossed behind my back, attached to my neck with extra-strong army-issue duct tape. She runs the rest of the tape from my wrists between my legs, across my left shoulder and back to my fingertips. The same again over my right shoulder. When she pulls it off, I'd say we'll be back to the roots with the whole skinning thing. None of this has the slightest thing in common with a coming-of-age drama. To make sure skin doesn't decompose once it's been separated from an organism, you tan it. Using potassium cyanide and alum, dissolved in water and applied to the skin. It has to be stretched, that's the tanning process, and after a while it hardens, then you have to keep stretching it more and more, watching out that it doesn't tear of course. To be honest, though, I don't know if I really ought to do it myself, it's, well.

I won't need my hands anyway.

There are parts of me that she doesn't touch, that she has no access to.

As soon as I move half an inch, the tendons between my shoulder and my chest will tear.

Unfortunately, you can't inflict violence on her. She is silent, coupling lack of responsibility with patience, she is simply silent, absolutely and totally and entirely with her hidden, unpredictable preferences that always entice her a long, long way.

And that's a storm that turns me into a desert. A very quiet storm. I listen solely to her silence, I tell her I have to bleed, I learn from all her weaknesses and follow her to the ends of the earth.

She prompts curiosity. She's just killing it right now.

Are we talking about feelings here? Is there any call for feelings? What can be born of me, for her?

There is something terrible about imagining that I am forced to feel something I'm unaware of. That she's binding me to impulses I have no notion of.

I don't notice that she turns me away from myself. She doesn't demand any attention from me, nor the slightest thought. All she gives is limitless distraction.

The reverse of faith, which isn't doubt but ignorance and neglect.

She isn't addressing me. She isn't actually addressing anyone; I've come that far now. She doesn't talk to herself and she has no listener. The vaster and yet more singular existence of a changeable nucleus listens to her, almost too general, as though what a moment ago was 'I', confronting her, awakened into a 'we', presence and united force of a common spirit. I am a little more, a little less than myself. More, in any case, than all people.

In this 'we' there is the earth, the power of the elements, a sky that is not this sky, there is a feeling of loftiness and calm, there is also the bitterness of an obscure constraint.

All this is 'I' before her, and she seems almost nothing at all.

I stare at her mouth, at the mattress, at the sunrise, at the forty-two missed calls. If I ever die maybe something of me will be left over. And then the whole dirty lot will rot away. Or maybe not. To be honest I don't think about it. I have enough problems already, and if I start thinking about life after death – come on. It's all too complicated and esoteric for me.

'Why esoteric? Death is death, what's esoteric about that?'

'True.'

And that's the last thing we share. I cry when you bleed. And I bleed when you cry. I don't lie to you. I love what you are. I'll do all I can to give you all I can. And I can always tell by your eyes where you've been. Your eyes. Your eyes. Your eyes. Your eyes. And you say, 'Your family was right. You're scum that we could only get rid of through silence.'

Dear Mifti,

I see the sin in your grin. In the shape of your mouth. All I want is to see you in terrible pain. Though we won't ever meet again I'll remember your name.

I can't believe you were once like everybody else. You're not a child any more, you're like the devil himself. You're scum that we can only get rid of through silence. I pray to God I can think of a nice thing to say about you. But I don't think I can any more.

You're scum, darling, you're like scabies, and I hope you know that the cracks in your smile are starting to show. Now the world needs to see that it's time for you to go. There's no light in your eyes and your brain is so slow. I bet you sleep like a baby with your thumb in your mouth. I could melt at the idea of putting a gun in there. It makes me sick when I hear all the shit that you talk. There's a space kept for you in hell. A seat with your name on it. When you look in the mirror do you see what I see? And if you do, why the fuck, WHY ARE YOU STILL LOOKING AT ME?

Your mother

Thanks to:

Coco, Jonas Weber Herrera, Tjorven Vahldieck, Annika Pinske, Kathrin Krottenthaler, Jule Böwe, Christian Fenske, Juri, Christiane Voss, Laura Tonke, René Pollesch, Leo and Jan, Maurice Blanchot, Ulrike Ostermeyer, Petra Eggers, Sophie Rois, Gabriel, Leisha, Maren Ade, Maria, Pascal Laugier, Airen and, above all, Carl Hegemann.

Particular thanks to Kathy Acker.

The following sources (books, songs, films, blogs etc.) have been flowed into the text as verbatim quotes, modified quotes or inspiration:

Airen, *Strobo*, with an epilogue by BOMÉC, © 2009 SuKulTur, Berlin.

Further sources (in part modified and dispersed over longer passages):

Kathy Acker, *My Mother: Demonology* (Grove Press, 1994), © 1993 Kathy Acker; *Blood and Guts in High School Plus Two* (Macmillan, 1984); *Great Expectations* (Grove Press, 1993), © 1992 Kathy Acker; Paul Arden, *Whatever You Think, Think the Opposite* (Penguin Books, 2006), © 2006 Paul Arden; Maurice Blanchot, *Le dernier homme* (Editions Gallimard, 1957), © Maurice